Best wishes! Marilyn Baxter

WHAT A DAY!

SHORT STORIES BY SOUTHERN WRITERS

To Keela Best always – Linda Howard

MARILYN BAXTER   BETTY BOLTÉ   BONNIE GARDNER

LINDA HOWARD   LINDA WINSTEAD JONES

CRYSTAL R. LEE   LESLIE SCOTT   JANNETTE SPANN

CARLA SWAFFORD   CS WARD   TOM WINSTEAD

Betty Bolté

Keela, Best wishes and happy reading! Crystal R. Lee

Leslie Scott

Bonnie Gardner

Best wishes! CS Ward

HEART OF DIXIE FICTION WRITERS

FOREWORD

The collection of short stories in this anthology are all written by members of Heart of Dixie Fiction Writers. We are writers who cover the gamut of experience and genre, from multi-published to unpublished, from romance to science fiction, from young adult to fantasy. As a group we are open to all writers of fiction, supporting one another along the never-ending path of learning and developing our craft.

We hope you enjoy these stories.

Linda Howard

MYSTIC MATCHMAKER

LINDA WINSTEAD JONES

Three days until the summer solstice.

Tobias was her last hope.

Helen purposely didn't look toward her two good friends, Ginger and Ramona, as she made her way past occupied tables in the ground floor dining hall of the facility she'd called home for the past several years. Tonight's supper was chicken and rice, served with green beans, peaches, and homemade rolls. Those she passed on her way to the table by the window seemed to be enjoying their meals. Even Ginger and Ramona, the traitors, she could tell even though she didn't look directly at them. She wouldn't give them the satisfaction. She could see them well enough out of the corner of her eye.

The three friends had eaten their meals at that same table together for years, since Ramona had moved into The Egg—The Mystic Springs Home for the Exceptionally Gifted, the retirement home for Springers who didn't dare settle down elsewhere in their old age, these days—and they would all share meals there again. But she wasn't ready to forgive them. Not yet.

There wasn't much that could come between the old friends. Mystic Springs was a small town, and like other small towns it was filled with secrets the residents gladly kept. True, their secrets could not be called *typical*. No, their secrets involved witches, good and bad; shifters, who could cause a ruckus when it suited them; and magic that often surprised even the oldest Springer. Helen wasn't exactly the oldest Springer in this room, but she was getting pretty darn close to it.

Her chin lifted a bit. No matter what bound the three friends together, not everything could be easily forgiven. She was *not* an interfering biddy. She *didn't* have to mind her own business, not where family was concerned. Minding her own business had never been her strong suit. Why start now?

Tobias was eating alone this evening. Helen didn't know where his brother Vince was at the moment, but she decided to take his absence as a gift. The fewer people who were in on her plan, the better.

Too many cooks in the kitchen, and all that.

"May I join you?" she asked, standing by Tobias's table with tray in hand.

He'd been intent on his supper and was startled by her appearance, and by her question. After a short hesitation, he stood as a gentleman should. "Of course. I'd be pleased to have your company."

Helen put her tray down; Tobias held her chair out for her, then eased her closer to the table. The Harper brothers did have good manners. Tobias's hands were strong but they did show his age, in wrinkles and scars and a knot or two. Still, at the moment she concentrated on the strength she saw there, not the flaws.

"Where's Vince this evening?" she asked, because she

supposed she should. Tobias was being polite, after all. She should do the same before she attempted to rope him into...

No, there would be no roping. She'd persuade him to assist her in her scheme...

No, not a scheme, a plan. A loving, well-intentioned...

"Vince doesn't like rice. He decided to walk down the street to the cafe for a burger tonight."

Right to it, then. "Do you remember my niece, Arminda?"

Her dinner companion looked puzzled for a moment, then a light of remembrance came to his eyes. "Of course. She left town right out of high school, didn't she? Pretty girl. Went by Armi, as I recall."

Helen pursed her lips. Arminda was a lovely name; a feminine, proper, family name. Armi was, well, it sounded as if her niece should be wearing clunky boots and camo. "Yes. Bless her heart." Helen paused to take a bite of her chicken and rice. It wasn't as good as hers, but by golly she hadn't had to cook it, either. She considered that a fair tradeoff.

Tobias looked concerned. The blessing could've been one of censure or sympathy. Sometimes it was hard to tell.

Helen swallowed her chicken and rice and took a sip of water before saying, "Arminda is coming to town for the summer solstice and festival this year."

"That's a surprise," Tobias said. "She hasn't been to Mystic Springs in years, has she?"

"She hasn't come for a visit since she married that man from Tennessee, more than twenty years ago. I'm sorry to say she's divorced, now, bless her heart." Two blessings within a few minutes, but that was the state of Arminda's life these days. Divorced, fifty, angry, and starting over in all the wrong ways.

She needed help, that much was clear.

Tobias shook his head, took a bite of his casserole, and nodded wisely. He seemed to be considering poor Arminda's

3

state of affairs for a moment that went on too long. "Do you think your niece might consider staying in Mystic Springs?"

"I wish she would, but she's made the foolish decision to invest her savings in a business more than an hour away, near Angel Lake."

"There's not much going on in those parts," Tobias said with evident concern.

"There is not. I don't know why…"

Well, maybe she did know. Arminda had no magic, despite her fine, powerful heritage. She couldn't read minds, move objects, or shift into an animal at will or at the demand of the moon, and she'd never shown any indication of skill with potions or spells. She might as well be a Non-Springer. Arminda had never felt as if she belonged here, bless her…

No, no more blessing. Time to get busy.

"I've been thinking," Helen said in an almost nonchalant voice. "If by chance we can find Arminda a man, a Mystic Springs man, and set a grand romance into motion while she's here for the festival, she might rethink her foolish decisions."

Tobias scanned the crowd in the dining hall. "What would she think of an older man?"

"Not much, I'm afraid." There was no chance of igniting a hot, life-changing romance in a single day, not with one of the residents of The Egg. No, they needed someone, well, hotter. "I was thinking maybe that Lovell fellow might suit. He's a bit young for her, but other than that I think they'd be well suited."

Tobias was not convinced. His face made that clear. "Maybe you're looking at this in the wrong way. Armi might be interested in settling down, now that's she's fifty. Maybe you could get her interested in your book club, or the knitting group."

"Unlikely," Helen said. Arminda probably did read, but knitting? Not her style.

Helen took a deep breath, leaned forward a bit, and reached out a hand she placed over Tobias's. "I need your help. I have three days to come up with a plan. How can I convince Arminda to give up her foolish Angel Lake venture and stay here in Mystic Springs, where she belongs?"

Tobias squirmed. Was it the idea of helping her interfere that made him uneasy or was it her hand over his? She removed her hand as if the gesture had meant nothing. And it hadn't, of course.

"Why don't you get Ginger and Ramona to help you out?" he suggested. "You three are always thick as thieves, and when you put your heads together…"

"They think I'm being an interfering busybody, that I should mind my own business." She scoffed. "Since when have I been any good at minding my own business?"

He agreed to think about it, and she deemed that good enough. With that settled, she dug into her chicken and rice. Yes, it tasted all the better because she hadn't had to cook it.

Two days until the summer solstice.

While the walk from The Egg to the busiest section of Mystic Springs downtown wasn't particularly far, for Helen's legs the walk was a bit much. Tobias was still quite strong, in spite of his advanced years, and though he did move more slowly than he once had, he made the walk with or without his brother a couple days a week. It would take her hours to make what should be a twenty minute walk, with all the stops to rest she'd have to make along the way. Her companion was kind enough not to point that out as they stepped onto the bus for a short ride.

The Egg bus took them to Eve's Cafe, where they had pie and coffee. They needed to come up with a plan, of sorts, in a place where their neighbors, friends, and relatives couldn't overhear. As they ate their pie they talked about other things. His brother Vince, who thought they were misguided, as Ginger and Ramona continued to do. The number of new residents in town. They were in the midst of a real population surge. The weather, which had turned hot in the past month. Magic offered Springers many gifts, but some things were inevitable. Summer heat was one of them.

After they ate, they walked across the street to the library. Helen wanted the newest thriller from her favorite author, and Tobias had a book to return. It was a non-fiction book; history. It didn't take long to discover that the book she wanted wasn't yet available. Just as well. She wouldn't have a lot of time for reading until after she'd handled the Arminda crisis.

Helen wandered away from the front desk to look up and down the library aisles as Tobias chatted with the librarian, Marnie Maxwell. It was a long shot, but she hoped to spot a handsome, fiftyish, well-read man who would blow Arminda's socks off.

Her hopes were quickly dashed.

They said goodbye to Marnie, and Tobias opened the door for Helen. They stepped onto the sidewalk, out of the air-conditioning and into the heat. "Maybe we'll have better luck in the antiques store," she suggested, and they turned in that direction. Quite a few Springers had returned to town in the past eight months, since what was commonly called the night of the fall. It hadn't been a fall, exactly, but the events of that night had definitely changed things.

Her grandson Travis, Chief of Police, had hired a couple of officers to help him, thanks to fatherhood as well as increased activity in their small town. Helen deemed both men too young for Arminda, and Tobias agreed.

She kept coming back to Nelson Lovell. Would Arminda go

for a Bigfoot shifter? The man was handsome enough—in his human form—even if he was occasionally a jerk.

Two young boys, elementary school age she judged, ran toward them. They laughed and shouted and one boy pushed at the other. Heathens. "Oh," she said, the thought coming to her as she studied the young miscreants, "maybe one of the older Milhouse boys..."

One of the kids took a sharp turn in her direction. Tobias responded quickly and efficiently, taking her hand, moving her aside, and placing himself between her and the child.

"Watch where you're going, young man," Tobias said sternly. Then he leaned down, taking the child's shoulder in what appeared to be an iron grip. "Apologize to the lady."

"Sorry," the boy said. Maybe he even meant it. It was hard to tell.

Tobias released his hold and the kids skipped on.

"Forget the antiques store," Tobias said. He took her hand again and held on. Interesting. It felt... nice. "How about ice cream?"

"We just had pie!" she argued.

"So? Life is short. We should eat all the ice cream, pie, cupcakes, and cookies we desire."

He had a point. "I have so much work to do."

Tobias stopped in the middle of the sidewalk. He didn't release her hand and she didn't draw it back, but he turned to look at her full on. "You don't yet have a plan. Hoping to stumble across a man your niece might fall instantly in love with isn't likely to work."

"But..."

"If you want to entice Armi to move back to Mystic Springs, it's going to take more than a man, I suspect."

He did make some sense. "I haven't told you, but..." Helen looked this way and that, then leaned in close to say, "The busi-

7

ness ventures in Angel Lake? She's buying a ratty hotel and a... a *bar*." It was so unseemly.

Tobias smiled. "So she's not looking for a man, she's looking for her own business."

He really did have a nice smile, she conceded. Silently, to herself, of course. "I suppose that's true," she said.

They resumed their walk toward the ice cream shop. "Ice cream, then back home," he said. "Come to my room tonight after dinner and we'll put our heads together."

"I can't possibly..."

"Of course you can," he interrupted. "If you sneak up to the third floor after eight, no one will see you. And if they do..." He shrugged his shoulders. "Tell them I made cookies."

"I suppose..."

He squeezed her hand. "I'll help you all I can, Helen."

For the first time in days, Helen smiled. She wasn't alone. If she was a busybody, so was Tobias Harper.

One day until the summer solstice.

A bed and breakfast wasn't all that much different from a motel. Once Arminda saw the Riverside Bed and Breakfast, she'd be sold. It was much preferable to her current plan. Fingers crossed Arminda would agree.

She'd made her way to Tobias's room last night, as he'd suggested. They'd had cookies and herbal tea, and had conspired like two old friends whose minds were working in concert. She hadn't given up on Lovell, not entirely, but as Tobias had suggested that might not be what Arminda wanted or needed.

She should know what her niece needed, as she often—

sometimes—knew what others needed. Sadly she was drawing a blank, magically speaking.

Helen had barely slept, after she'd returned to her own room. She blamed her restlessness on all the sugar she'd consumed. Pie, ice cream, and cookies, all in one day! Today if Tobias suggested more sweets, she'd refuse. She could be disciplined, when she had to be.

For today's trip to town, Tobias had borrowed a friend's car. Sitting in the passenger seat while he drove down quiet Mystic Springs streets, she felt like a girl again. A girl on a date with her fella. Silly thought, though Tobias did look quite dapper today. It was mere coincidence that she'd spent a little more time on her hair and makeup today, and had reached past other options for a pretty dress adorned with lavender flowers.

He parked as near the B&B front porch as possible, and hurried around the vehicle to her side of the car to open her door and offer a hand. Together, they walked toward the big white house.

"What if Molly doesn't want to sell?" Tobias asked in a lowered voice.

"I can be very persuasive."

He smiled at that. "Yes, you can." He took her hand again as she put one foot on the bottom step, simply to support her, she was sure, though she did like the feel of his hand in hers. He might be old and gray-haired and not as strong as he'd once been, but there was strength in his steadying hand.

She hadn't been able to persuade Ginger and Ramona to help her, but she was no longer angry with them for that failing. If they'd agreed, she never would've had such a fine partner in Tobias.

They didn't bother to knock. There were several semi-regular residents of the bed and breakfast; they came and went at all hours of the day—between 8 in the morning and 7 or so at night—making the front parlor basically a public space. There was another selling point for Arminda; built-in customers. Nelson Lovell was one of those who was in residence more often than not.

She hadn't given up on introducing the two to see if there were sparks. There was an age difference, but these days that didn't seem to mean much at all.

Would Arminda have an issue with a Bigfoot shifter as a beau? Some women did, sad to say.

Helen made her way toward the kitchen with Tobias beside her, still holding her hand.

Molly was surprised when Helen stuck her head in the kitchen and called a friendly woo-hoo. The startled innkeeper jumped a little and dropped the pan she'd been washing in the sink.

She smiled when she saw her visitors. "Hey, you two. What brings you here?"

Molly was awfully friendly for a woman who'd... well, she had not been forgiven for her bad judgment, at least not by most in town. A wise woman would be happy to sell and get out.

No one had ever accused Molly Duncan of being wise.

"My niece is coming to town for the solstice, and I was wondering..."

Molly stopped the conversation with a raised hand. "I'm completely booked for the week. Between my regulars and a few relatives coming in for a couple of days, every room is occupied."

Helen pursed her lips. She did not like to be interrupted. "I was going to ask if you'd ever thought of selling the Riverside Bed and..."

"Hell no!" Molly said sharply, then she laughed. "Why would I sell when I just invested so much in remodeling and I'm finally making a profit?"

Because no one likes you? Because by all rights you should

be in jail? Because any self-respecting woman would've snuck out of town on her own months ago?

Helen smiled. "Just a passing thought," she said, hoping her expression didn't give away her real feelings. It was likely a false hope, since she'd never been good at hiding her feelings.

"Anything else?" Molly asked, as she headed for the back of the room and a closet there. She started pulling out cleaning supplies. This was still, as far as Helen knew, a one-woman operation. "With a full house, I've got to get busy."

"No, nothing else. I'll see you tomorrow at the festival." Everyone would be there. Even Molly.

Tobias led her down the hall and to the parlor. He was headed for the door, but Helen tugged on his hand and pointed to a comfortable looking wing chair.

"Oh," he said, concern in his voice. "Do you need to sit?"

"I do," she said, lowering herself. "I'm not weak or tired," she explained, "but I need a moment to think. If I can't find an appropriate man or a ready-made business for Arminda, how can I convince her to stay?"

Tobias didn't sit. He stood before her, crossed his arms over his chest, and said, "Maybe you can't. Maybe you're not supposed to."

Ginger and Ramona had told her the same thing and it had made her so angry. But for some reason, hearing the words from Tobias didn't rile her. "My powers have been fading, but I'm supposed to know what she needs. It's my gift, it's what makes me a Springer. It's an ability I passed to my son and to my grandsons, in one form or another, but when it comes to Arminda… I want to help her and I don't know how."

Tobias smiled. The sun slanted through the front window and hit him at a funny angle so that for a moment he looked like a young man, in his prime, handsome and fit.

When he and Vince had moved into The Egg, they'd been inundated with female visitors. For the first six months, they'd been the recipients of cakes, cookies, pies... casseroles, even though three meals a day were provided in the dining hall. Helen and her pals had scorned these women and had dubbed them the Casserole Brigade. Obviously the women of the brigade had been trying to corral one of the few eligible men residing in The Egg. Some of them likely had hanky-panky on their minds. Hussies.

When it became clear the Harper brothers were perfectly happy remaining single the Casserole Brigade had dwindled, one hot dish at a time.

Helen had never delivered so much as a crumb to either brother. Such a display of desperation was beneath her. Now she wondered if maybe she should've made an effort...

The light changed once more, and the Tobias she knew so well was himself once again. Given his age, he was still quite handsome.

She offered her hand; he took it and assisted her to her feet. As he opened the front door, Tobias said, "I meant to tell you earlier, that dress you're wearing today is lovely. Very flattering. I hope you don't mind that I say so," he added quickly.

Helen smiled as she stepped onto the front porch of the B&B that would not solve her Arminda problem. "Not at all," she said, glancing over her shoulder to smile at her escort. "Not at all."

The Summer Solstice

The residents of The Egg had all loaded onto the bus right after lunch to make the trip to town. It would take more than one trip to ferry them all there and back again. Helen sat next to Tobias on the full bus, while Ginger and Ramona took their places directly behind them. Helen even smiled at her friends.

How could she stay angry when things were working out so well? Not that she had a solution to the Arminda issue, but still, the last few days had been lovely, in so many ways.

Vendors were set up along Main Street, some of them selling wares, others giving away samples. Springers and Non-Springers alike visited, shopped, and ate. The Milhouse brothers band was set up at the far end of the street, not far from the library, playing some godawful modern music. Something they called Skynyrd. Thank goodness they were at a distance, and the music was muted.

Luke's wife, the lovely Jordan, had called upon her magic to direct clouds overhead to block the worst of the sun. It was still a warm day, but the clouds and a nice breeze made all the difference.

Parking for the visitors was less than ideal, since Main Street was blocked off for pedestrian traffic. Anyone coming in from beyond Mystic Springs, as Arminda would, had to veer into a neighborhood on the west side of town and park on the street, then walk to Main Street. Helen kept an eye out for her niece, but an hour passed, then another, and there was no sign of her.

Maybe Arminda had changed her mind. Maybe all her planning and scheming had been for nothing!

She glanced at Tobias. Well, not for nothing. She'd made a new friend.

There were folding chairs placed in front of businesses up and down the street. After a while, Helen found one in the shade and sat. Tobias sat beside her. They ate ice cream and talked about their favorite television shows. They were both obsessed with a singing show, where previously unknown talent was on display, and a reality show she'd been embarrassed to admit to anyone she watched. Tobias watched it too, every week. People could surprise you...

Ginger and Ramona joined them, after a while. The four of them sat in the shade and ate sweets and watched people walk by. Vince came along after a while and sat next to Ramona, who was seated at the far end.

Vince liked the Skynyrd, and sometimes sang along. There was no accounting for taste... Though she did like the one about sweet home Alabama. It was quite catchy.

Just as Helen was about to give up, she saw Arminda and Travis, the cousins smiling and talking as they crossed the street, weaving around children who didn't look where they were going.

Poor Arminda, her life had taken such a dark turn...

As Helen watched, she noticed that her niece was smiling. Arminda looked good for a woman just turned fifty, and while some of her recent emails had been tinged with anger—and rightly so—she looked... fine. Happy, even.

Helen, who always knew what others needed, had an epiphany.

Arminda needed her aunt to leave her the hell alone.

"Armi's been looking for you," Travis said as he directed his cousin to his Nana. "I should've known you and your cohorts would be hiding in the shade."

"I'm hardly hiding," Helen said as she stood to give her niece a proper hug. "It's so good to see you."

"Nice to see you, too," Arminda said. They separated, and the younger woman looked up and down Main Street. "Not much has changed in Mystic Springs, but it does seem to be more crowded than the last time I was here."

"Which was much too long ago," Helen said, a gentle jab. "I've... I've missed you." Enough sentimentality. "So," she said, lifting her chin slightly. "Angel Lake."

Arminda nodded. "Yes. I have so much work to do to get everything ready to open. The previous owner didn't even bother to dust, much less renovate."

After bemoaning her niece's choices for the past couple of weeks, Helen had to work a bit to say, in a somewhat sincere voice, "Well, I wish you the best of luck."

Arminda did look a bit surprised, but pleasantly so. She knew her aunt well. She was soon joined by two women friends who'd come along for the day, and after introductions had been made the three women strolled down the street, paying proper attention to the booths and tables of wares, and to the music. On occasion, the shortest one danced along the sidewalk.

Ginger and Ramona decided to walk to the end of the street, and Vince offered to escort them. They moved slower than Arminda and her friends, but they did move.

"I suppose I might as well go home," Helen said to Tobias. "This was a foolish plan. I'm no matchmaker, and Arminda doesn't need one." She sighed. "Armi doesn't need me to interfere in her life." If her niece preferred a shortened version of her lovely name, then her aunt should respect that choice. "I should've abandoned this idea before I got started."

"I'm glad you didn't," Tobias said.

"You're just being polite. I dragged you into my silly scheme, put you to so much trouble…"

"It was no trouble," he said. He sounded sincere, but then she could manage that herself, no matter how put out she might be.

"Let's go for a walk before we head back to The Egg." He offered his arm and she took it, and they followed in the path of the relatives and friends who'd preceded them.

It was nice to walk in the shade, to stop now and then to sample chocolate or cookies or Jordan's ice cream. The small cup, of course. While they ate ice cream, the band took a short break. Helen relished the silence. She loved music, but she was very particular. Raucous had never been her style.

They were far too close to the stage where the band would continue to play well into the night when the musicians returned. The five werewolf brothers took up their instruments, spoke amongst themselves, and laughed. Helen turned, intent on getting as far away as possible before they started making noise again.

But Tobias took her arm and stilled her. "Not yet," he said in a lowered voice.

"I'm really not..."

He looked her in the eye. "Not yet."

The singer, red-headed Weston, took to the microphone for a short announcement. "We have a special request to start this set. Not our usual thing, but I think we can pull it off."

Helen recognized the song right away. Her favorite; Unchained Melody.

Tobias led her into the street, where people had been dancing all afternoon, and as they reached the middle of the street he asked, "May I have this dance?"

Helen held her breath. She hadn't danced in years! She wasn't sure she could dance! What if she stumbled and fell, or stepped on Tobias's foot, or reeled into a dancer beside or behind her? She wasn't even sure she was capable of reeling, anymore. But she found herself letting Tobias hold her in a dancer's embrace as she whispered, "I'd love to."

Weston Milhouse might not be a Righteous Brother, but he did a more than acceptable job. Tobias held her while they danced gently, easily, and with a lovely rhythm. No longer in the shade, the late afternoon sun made her squint a bit. The light shimmered, her vision blurred and then cleared, and she saw Tobias not as he was now, but as he'd once been. Young. Strong. Straight and steady. As in that brief moment in the B&B yesterday, there were no wrinkles on his face; his hair was dark and full. And the smile... oh, the smile.

"You look..." She stopped. It was ridiculous. She was having a stroke. Maybe a nearby witch was having some fun with her. It was a dream! The entire day had been...

No. It was real, somehow. Some way.

"You look different," she said as he swung her around. Her

legs didn't feel at all stiff; she was no longer in danger of stumbling or falling.

"Younger, perhaps?" he asked with a smile.

She nodded. "It's like I'm seeing you through different eyes, through a sheen of..." She couldn't say it. Love? Magic? Enchantment?

"It's about time," Tobias said. "It's how I've always seen you, Helen. It's how I see you every day. You are without a doubt the most beautiful woman I've ever known."

She hadn't been beautiful for a long time, but as they danced in the street she felt as if she could be. No, as if she *was*, at least to Tobias.

"Did you request this song?" she asked. "It's my favorite."

Tobias's smile faded a bit. "No, it wasn't me."

Coincidence? She didn't believe in such a thing. She believed in fate, magic, and family, but coincidence was a bridge too far.

Tobias swung her around and she saw them. Ramona and Ginger stood just a few feet away, Vince between them. All three were smiling like the troublemakers they were.

No, not troublemakers. Matchmakers.

The song ended. The dance came to a close. Tobias leaned in and down and gave Helen a short—but not too short—kiss. People would stare, she knew it, but at this moment she didn't care. She hadn't been kissed properly in a very long time.

As they separated, she expected Tobias to return to his usual appearance. He was a handsome old man, so it wasn't as if she'd complain when whatever enchantment made him appear to be a young man ended. But it didn't end. Maybe later. Maybe not.

He took her arm and guided her to the sidewalk. Helen caught a glimpse of herself, and him, in their reflection in the antiques store window. They were both young again. She was even thinner and taller, by a bit. How was that possible? Did Tobias really always see her this way? Someone stepped in front of her, passing by as they headed to the end of the street, getting in the way and ruining the picture.

She felt a bit of stiffness returning to her legs, which was to be expected. The reflection in the window now showed her in all her aged glory. But for a while, for a few precious moments, she'd felt young again. Truth be told, in her head she always felt the same. It was her body—and her mirror—that occasionally betrayed her.

"Well, that was lovely," Ramona said as the three matchmakers pulled up beside the dancers.

"Very nice," Ginger said. "Why, for a few seconds I could've sworn you were both thirty years younger!"

"Forty," Vince said, a smile in his voice.

"There's magic in music, especially here in Mystic Springs," Helen said, not bothering to confront her friends with accusations of interference. Not here and now. Had they planned this all along? Had Vince been in on the matchmaking from the start?

She'd thank her friends later. And get details. From one busybody to another… she was curious about their planning.

"It's time for me to head home," she said, "but I need to stop at the grocery store first."

"The grocery store!" Ramona said, horror in her voice. "Why?"

Helen looked up to Tobias, who continued to hold her arm. Maybe he wasn't quite as handsome as he'd been a few moments ago, but the smile was the same. It was charming and real, and intended for her.

She smiled herself. "I have a hankering to make a casserole."

The End

ABOUT LINDA

Linda Winstead Jones is the New York Times and USA Today bestselling author of more than eighty romance novels and novellas across several sub-genres. She's easily distracted (Look! A squirrel!) and writes the stories that speak to her in the moment. Paranormal. Romantic Suspense. Twisted Fairy Tales. Cowboys. Her books are for readers who want to escape from reality for a while, who don't mind the occasional trip into another world for a laugh, a chill, the occasional heartwarming tear. Where will we go next?

Sign up for Linda's newsletter at
www.lindawinsteadjones.com

A HARVEST MOON TO REMEMBER

CRYSTAL R. LEE

Minerva spun on bare feet, arms flung out to her sides with wild abandon. The evening of the Harvest Moon had finally arrived! Its appearance two days before the autumnal equinox marked the last full moon of summer.

Excitement charged the air, raising goosebumps on her nape as she glanced out the window of her hidden haven on Goat Island. Located in Honeycomb Cove, part of Lake Guntersville in northern Alabama, her special hideaway provided the solitude she craved to balance the stresses of life. She also enjoyed taking the sixty-foot plunge into the water from the highest cliff on the island. That's how she had met fellow thrill-seeker Christian Davenport, the wealthy thirty-something widower with mysterious dark eyes and jet-black hair, soon to be her hot date. His yacht should pull into the cove within the hour.

Minerva sat down at the old vanity nestled in an alcove to put the finishing touches on her makeup, then elevated her chin to inspect her handiwork in the oval mirror. Curled lashes framed large lavender eyes staring out from a narrow face with soft hollows beneath prominent cheekbones. She had been told her flawless, pale complexion appeared ethereal, particularly at night. It had certainly worked to her advantage over the years. She picked up the ornate brush and eased it through the water-fall of hair cascading over her shoulders. When the strands shone like spun silver, she replaced the brush on the weathered surface and heaved a sigh.

The day would be a complete success if she could get darling Chris to open up more about his past, namely the circumstances surrounding his late wife's death. Whenever she mentioned it, he clammed up, his face an impenetrable mask. The woman had been dead over a year now. Given his known amorous activity during the majority of that period, he no longer mourned her loss. Besides, she had it on good authority he harbored secrets in need of confession. Such a pity to tarnish what had developed between them, but her soul demanded the truth from his lips. Honesty above all, even love. Not the most romantic notion, but necessary for survival.

Perhaps the Harvest Moon would shine the light on truth.

As she considered her predicament, Minerva lifted a trea-sured shell necklace from the right-hand drawer of the vanity and fastened it around her neck. The hoard of delicate white clam shells hung to her waist, each a representative of her many conquests, their names and faces forever preserved in her mind. She straightened, head held high. Wearing it instilled confi-dence, a sense of power and control.

Her bow-shaped mouth slid into a smile that reached her eyes.

There was always room for one more.

Standing, Minerva snapped on mother-of-pearl bangles, smoothed a glistening silver sheath over her svelte curves, and slipped her feet into matching low-heeled sandals. She pirou-etted before the full-length mirror on the opposite wall of the alcove.

"Mirror, mirror," she said, batting her lashes. "Darling Chris won't know what hit him."

Satisfied with reflected perfection, she stepped out into the night.

———————

Christian pulled into Honeycomb Cove, then stationed his fifty-two-foot Hatteras *Spiritsong* a safe distance from the Goat Island cliffs and deployed the anchor. Why had Minerva asked him to pick her up from the island? Oh, yeah, something about the Harvest Moon. Still, with no houses there, no amenities of any kind, the choice seemed odd. He'd much rather wine and dine her on board at the marina. Shore power provided a quieter atmosphere than running the generator, especially since his needed an overhaul. They could also take a moonlit stroll along the dock.

He engaged the remote spotlight and panned the area. Several bats darted over the bow. At least, they looked like bats in the split-second he saw them. No visible signs of anyone else nearby. Assuming Minerva was here, how had she arrived? Certainly not by a boat she'd piloted. *Spiritsong* was the only vessel in the vicinity.

Christian killed the engines and glanced at his watch. Twenty minutes until the appointed hour of eleven o'clock. Not quite the Witching Hour in this region. He raked a hand through his hair and chuckled. Maybe she was a witch, traveling by broom, her timing an attempt to throw him off the scent. Keep him guessing. She might be lurking in the trees, watching his every move. The thought sent a shiver down his spine.

With no time to waste, he shook off the sensation, raced down the steps leading from the flybridge, and darted into the salon to check the control panel. Satisfied the proper switches were engaged, he closed the door to the control panel and whipped around the counter into the galley for items to set the scene. Ambiance mattered to Minerva, but he wanted to keep it simple. Armed with tableware, a battery-operated candle, and a pillow for her chair, he returned to the enclosed aft deck to set the table to the sound of water breaking against the hull. He placed two white melamine plates, folded paper dinner napkins, and flatware on opposite sides of the teak surface, with the activated candle in the center. The food must wait until their return.

He consulted his watch. Ten minutes to spare. Not bad.

One last thing: the gift.

He retrieved the blue envelope from the salon and slid it beneath his plate. He had been carrying it around for two weeks. Such a formidable gift demanded the perfect moment, not to mention the perfect woman. Although Minerva seemed to fit the bill, he still had doubts. She had a peculiar manner that made the hair on the back of his neck stiff more than he cared to admit.

Hmm... Christian cocked his head and flexed his eyebrows. Maybe she was a witch.

Well, witch or not, a little mystery kept the relationship interesting.

Right?

Hopefully, it didn't bode ill since theirs had grown rather serious in the two short months they'd been dating. But Minerva kept pressing for details about the death of his late wife, Sandy. Not unreasonable from a certain point of view, but invasive in a way that set him on edge, as if she suspected him of having done something wicked. Other than Sandy, the majority of his so-called relationships had lasted no longer than a few dates. He went through women like sand through a sieve. Sandy, however, had been a means to advancing his own financial platform as well as a romantic attachment to a powerful family. And he had been faithful to her, given the stakes. Her death had been an end to an era.

Then along came Minerva. Sleek, beautiful Minerva.

Stupid, stupid man. He'd let this thing go too far, too fast. Now she was asking probing questions about Sandy. His chest tightened beneath the weight of the one topic he'd rather not discuss. Period.

Why couldn't the past stay in the past?

Agitated, he sucked in a breath between clenched teeth and released it slowly, rolling his shoulders to relieve tension in his neck. All of this turmoil for a woman who refused to let him see where she lived. She wouldn't disclose her address. Whenever they went out, he had to meet her at a place of her choosing, and never the same place twice.

Talk about suspicious...

Come to think of it, she was tight-lipped about her job too, even after he had prattled on about his success as a financial advisor and investor. His internet searches and discreet queries about Minerva had yielded no results. Not a trace of her in known business circles and publications.

Maybe she was a spy working undercover for a top-secret organization.

Stupid, stupid man.

Mind spinning, Christian scratched the stubble on his chin. What was really going on? Maybe this wasn't the perfect moment nor she the perfect woman. Shaking the flurry of thoughts aside, he hurried to launch the dinghy for his jaunt to Goat Island. It wouldn't do to be late.

Minerva indulged a deep, cleansing breath. The scent of pine and moist earth wafted on a refreshing breeze that made her hungry for seafood. Good seafood. She had eaten nothing since breakfast: a large pumpkin-spice scone on her way to work. Her stomach growled in protest. Christian better have a tasty treat to offer.

She wandered along the familiar narrow trail padded with autumn leaves and pine needles, winding through the trees and bracken to the low-lying rock ledges near the lake's edge. The Harvest Moon had risen, bold and bright, its shimmering veil draping the landscape. What a glorious sight! Silver highlights danced on the water like the playful river sprites near her home. Frog-song filled the air as bats swooped high and low in search of their next meal. Overhead, an owl soared across the sky, a dark omen silhouetted against the moon.

Christian waited on the shore, lantern in hand, one foot propped on his dinghy to secure it. While water lapped against the small boat, he appeared to have no difficulty maintaining his balance. Not far away, his yacht sat at anchor in a luminous blue pool created by the vessel's underwater lights. Illuminated portions of the deck and flybridge created a magical aura against the backdrop of imposing shadows.

"Greetings, fair maiden." His husky tone made her belly quiver. Clad in shorts and a tropical camp shirt, Christian motioned with an outstretched hand. "Shall we? I hope you find the evening's entertainment enjoyable."

"I'm sure I will." Brushing strands of hair from her face, Minerva returned his smile with a slow blink to hold him in thrall. "I've been looking forward to seeing you all day."

He went still, as if entranced. His eyes never strayed from hers as she placed her hand in his, taking care not to stumble aboard the shifting dinghy. Unfortunately, their point of contact sparked another strange quiver in the pit of her stomach, upsetting her usual sense of grace and poise. And it wasn't hunger. Thankfully, the sensation passed the instant she pulled her hand away and fixed her gaze on the seat in the bow.

What was going on?

Normally men didn't have that effect on her. Only one man ever, in fact: Marco, the gorgeous philanthropist she had agreed to marry before he betrayed her. He had paid dearly for his unforgivable error in judgment.

Minerva clutched her shell necklace in a fist against her heart where Christian couldn't see it as she approached her seat. Betrayal of any kind could not—would not—be tolerated. That was why she kept him at arm's length when it came to matters of home and work. While she liked him, she didn't trust him enough to share that information. The risk was too great. As Chair of the Board of Directors of the Morrowvian Pearl Syndicate, she understood and enforced the rigorous, often ruthless, means necessary to protect trade secrets.

Christian held the vessel in place until she settled in the bow, then climbed in, took his seat behind the wheel at the console, and started the engine. They set off at a leisurely pace.

He cleared his throat, capturing her attention. "Do you mind if we make a side trip to the bat cave? I'd like to take a couple of pictures, see if I can capture anything up close this time."

The man fancied himself a professional photographer, having sold several photos to one of the boating magazines. Two years lapsed since his last sale, but he'd made sure to show her the spread one lazy afternoon over docktails at the marina.

"Of course." Minerva lowered her voice to a soft croon. "Perhaps you would take a few of the moon as well, to mark the occasion."

She observed his mechanical nod through lowered lashes.

"No problem. I'd be glad to."

Yes, an agreeable lover made the business of romance all the sweeter. As long as her desires and goals prevailed, she would ride the tide of darling Chris to her advantage, uncomfortable stomach flutters aside. Why not mix business with pleasure? While she had no desire to marry the guy—Marco's betrayal had sealed her fate against marriage—she worked hard to have the life of her dreams and deserved to have some fun. And he could be loads of fun, certainly worth the effort.

Christian stopped their craft about ten feet from the fenced-off entrance to the bat cave on the water and shut off the engine. Not far away, Guntersville Dam loomed in silence. No late-night commercial traffic locking through to disturb the peace. Always a plus.

After fumbling around in the bag at his feet, Christian retrieved a camera with a telephoto lens, put it in the proper mode, and began taking photos while Minerva stared up at the sky. Twinkling against the curtain of night, a scattering of stars surrounded the moon. With any luck his high-powered lens would capture a satisfactory image, preferably one which showcased the Harvest Moon's radiance.

A mild breeze carried the fresh scent and cool whisper of the lake, the air less humid in the last gasp of summer. Nevertheless, it clung to her flesh like a second skin. Minerva rubbed her bare arms and released a silent sigh. A moonlit swim was definitely on the agenda. Depending on the flow of events, it would make for a far better nightcap than alcohol.

"Seems I'm in luck," Christian said, shifting her focus. "I got what I came for." Brandishing his camera, he punctuated his wide grin with a playful wink, then capped the lens and returned the device to its bag. He winked again, his mouth quirked in a sly smile, and started the engine. "Harvest Moon indeed. Ready to move the party to *Spiritsong*, sweetheart?"

Christian didn't use terms of endearment often, so he must be in high spirits. Or have high expectations. Given their past encounters, the latter seemed part of his genetic code.

Minerva tilted her head and blew a kiss. "I thought you would never ask."

A wave of anticipation surged through her core as they closed the distance to the yacht.

Christian secured the dinghy to the transom and helped Minerva board *Spiritsong*, where she followed his lead and discarded her shoes just inside the transom door. Dainty purple toenails peeked out from the trailing hem of her gown as she entered the enclosed aft deck and proceeded to the table set for two. Turning, she nailed him with eyes the rich color of quality African amethyst, Sandy's favorite.

"You did this for me, darling Chris? How lovely."

Her voice washed over him, a luscious balm penetrating his very soul, rendering him mute. Her eyes appeared larger, their depths churning like waves crashing against a rocky shore at twilight. Stupefied, he just stared at her as a slow, calculating smile inched across her face, the type of smile a cunning witch might wear when luring you to your doom. He continued to linger, unmoving, as though waiting to be consumed.

After several seconds he snapped out of it and cleared his throat. "Y-yes, of course I did it for you. Who else would it be for?"

Minerva toyed with the shell necklace she wore. "Men are crafty creatures, capable of infinite subterfuge to get their way."

Her voice swept through him, a maelstrom reverberating in his ears. His breath hitched as she propped against the table, her full lips set in a resolute line.

"In the spirit of full disclosure, I must warn you that I will not tolerate betrayal. Any such act carries consequences."

Minerva's eyes grew darker than before, scary dark glaring out from her ghostly face, twin storms ready to unleash their fury. Christian shivered, suddenly cold. But it wasn't cold. No woman had ever affected him the way she did. Maybe she was a witch. Or a vampire.

Why did he keep entertaining nonsense?

Hell, maybe he was losing his mind.

With a quick shake of his head, Christian threw up his hands. "I assure you, betrayal is the last thing on my mind. I'm not Marco; I'm not lying in wait to break your heart. Nor do I plan to go the tragic route of your previous lover by drowning. I'm a very good swimmer, you see. So where's this coming from? Have I done something to make you doubt my intentions?"

"Not yet, Christian. But the night is young."

"I see."

"I doubt you do."

"Yes, I see quite clearly." Did he? Did he see anything clearly when near her? He pressed on before he forgot what he wanted to say. "The fact is you don't trust me. Am I right? Is that why you won't invite me to your house or tell me where you work? Are you afraid I might discover the secrets of your private life? Or do you fear I will profess my love and propose? Sorry. That last bit was out of bounds."

Minerva pushed away from the table and crooked a finger. "Let's not waste what remains of a magnificent evening."

Once again she refused to answer his questions. No surprise there. The storm in her eyes vanished, but an uncanny gleam smoldered in their cool lavender depths. She appeared the picture of angelic patience as she beckoned with her insistent finger, her luminous face framed by the silver splendor of her hair.

What now?

Hell, he would give her what she wanted, of course. Like usual. He seemed to lack a will of his own where she was concerned. Might as well surrender his soul. Minerva was special. She had captivated him from the beginning, despite his best efforts to keep things casual. Yeah, he would give her what she wanted and more.

What else could he do?

His movements resembled an automaton when he finally stepped forward and took her hand.

Minerva drew Christian into a tight embrace. Encircling his neck with her arms, she leaned against him, head back to hold his gaze. His body grew rigid, betraying his desire, while his heart hammered inside his muscular chest.

"That's better," she murmured.

Lacing her fingers behind his neck, Minerva forced him to dip his head for a slow kiss, parting his lips with her tongue, tasting him. Passion flared, driving the kiss deeper. Christian moaned, long and low in his throat, his claw-like fingers clutching her waist. His touch inflamed her spine, the sensation electric. Her heart raced alongside his, frantic.

Too frantic.

Too soon.

Pulling back, she ended the kiss, leaving him panting, eyes glazed.

"Oh, darling Chris." Minerva released a breathy laugh. "What does a girl have to do to get a drink around here?"

Absently, Christian shook his head. "Sorry, my bad. Adult beverages coming up." He combed his fingers through his hair and adjusted his shirt. "Please make yourself comfortable while I gather our feast."

Like a rat fleeing a sinking ship, he scampered through the door leading to the salon while she settled into the wicker chair with a pillow and surveyed the enclosed deck. Everything was neat and tidy. Impressive considering the hard work required to keep a boat clean and its contents organized. Christian maintained his yacht well.

Lavishly appointed, *Spiritsong* made a fine floating vacation home. They had already undertaken one three-week voyage to the Gulf of Mexico, touring marinas along the western coast of Florida, taking turns at the wheel, carefree, living the good life. With her at the helm, they had ventured about twenty-five miles offshore one day so he could fish and she could swim in the Gulf. Heavenly, the feel of salt water against bare flesh, the intoxicating smell of the ocean as the wind teased her hair.

Years ago, while residing in Florida, Minerva had obtained her captain's license in order to take people on chartered fishing expeditions. Since then, she had maintained her license and had acquired a fleet of four yachts reserved for the entertainment of a select clientele. A lucrative side venture she intended to exploit for maximum financial gain. Since she enjoyed riding the waves stationed at the helm, the controls at her fingertips, her heart, mind, and spirit at peace with the sea, she served as captain for chartered excursions whenever time permitted. She elevated her chin and smiled. Owning her own fleet never grew tiresome.

Christian's reappearance pulled her from her reverie. He cradled an uncorked bottle of champagne in the crook of one arm and a loaded tray secured by both hands, which he positioned at one end of the table. Minerva perused the contents: caviar with crème fraîche and blini, shrimp cocktail, grapes and strawberries, chocolate truffles. His feast did not disappoint.

Hair disheveled, his jaw clenched in concentration, he poured the champagne and thrust one of the flutes toward her, his hand shaking. Was he nervous? Worried? Addled? He certainly wasn't himself at the moment, but she pretended not to notice.

Minerva accepted the fragile glass, locking the stem between her thumb and first two fingers. "Thank you. You have selected all of my favorites."

Holding the flute aloft, she admired the effervescent liquid in the muted light. Then they toasted and sipped, his attention focused on the exit to her left. She observed his faraway look over the rim of her glass, giggling as the bubbles tickled her nose.

"Chris, darling, you seem preoccupied. Is something wrong?

Do you wish to escape?" Minerva set her champagne flute aside, propped her elbows on the table, and rested her chin on her hands. "Is there something you want to tell me?"

Christian fumbled with his plate, drumming his fingers along its edge, skewing it to reveal the tip of what appeared to be a piece of paper.

Curious, Minerva attempted to retrieve it. "What's under your plate?"

"All in good time." He caught her hand and kissed her fingers, his eyes shining with mischief. "Let's not spoil my little surprise just yet." He released her, then filled her plate with a small glass cup of shrimp cocktail, two blini loaded with caviar, and several strawberries.

"Will I like this surprise?"

"I hope so." Christian shoved a shrimp into his mouth, chased it with the rest of his champagne in one gulp, and exchanged the flute for a shot glass and the bottle of bourbon on the tray. "I'll be surprised if you don't." He poured a shot of the amber liquid, tossed it back, and repeated the operation.

What was darling Chris up to?

"What in the world can it be," Minerva crooned, dipping a shrimp in cocktail sauce and devouring it in one bite.

When Christian said nothing, she traced the side of his leg with her bare foot, studying him through lowered lashes. He fumbled his glass, nearly dropping it.

His lips curved into a lopsided grin. "That's cheating."

"All is fair in love and war." Minerva nibbled the blini with caviar and emptied her glass as she danced her foot up his leg and nestled it in his lap.

Wide-eyed, Christian squirmed and made a guttural sound. "You're such a bad girl."

Minerva kissed the air. "You have no idea."

With swift grace, she grasped the champagne bottle and refilled her glass, then eased the bottle onto the tray before pouring him a shot of bourbon. She wiggled her toes in his lap. Amused by his flushed cheeks, she withdrew her foot, popped a strawberry into her mouth, chewed and swallowed. Mmm, juicy and sweet, one of the best she'd had recently.

Then, weary of the tedious posturing, she heaved a sigh, flicked a strawberry across her plate, and glared at Christian. Time to steer the conversation to the heart of the matter.

"What draws you to a woman? Beauty, brains, or money? What drew you to Sandy?"

Christian frowned. "You know I don't like to talk about her."

"Indulge me." Hooking him with a slow blink, Minerva pitched her voice low and seductive. "She was not a casual fling. You married her, and if things had turned out differently, you would probably be married still. Right?"

At this point, he had inhaled a sufficient quantity of alcohol to render him agreeable to most any request. Darling Chris did love his bourbon though. He had a high tolerance for it.

Minerva selected a chocolate truffle, slid it between her lips, and leaned back, chewing and savoring the confection beneath his lingering stare, running her tongue along her bottom lip. "Am I right?"

With a sudden jolt, Christian straightened and raked a hand through his hair, as if remembering where he was. "Right. Well, Sandy was working a charity event when I first met her. By reputation, she was a very generous person, and I liked that about her. But prior to attending the event, I researched her background, family history and such. As it turned out, she was sitting on quite a nest egg, substantially more than my own meager fortune." He winked, his mouth twisting to one side.

Minerva stifled a laugh with a sip of champagne. She had it on good authority that his "meager fortune" was millions strong before he married Sandy. As for his late wife's family history, there was no way he had all the facts. Sandy's family had

33

connections to the Morrowvian Pearl Syndicate. She knew more about Sandy than he realized.

Christian swilled his bourbon before he continued, his smug grin showcasing straight white teeth. Handsome devil, even with the touch of gray in his stubble. So sure of himself.

"Indeed, Sandra Endicott was no slouch," he said, his tone matter-of-fact. "Like my folks, she came from old money, and being an only child, she inherited a vast fortune when her parents died in a plane crash. Needless to say, she insisted on a pre-nup before heading down the aisle."

"Smart woman."

"Hey, now."

Minerva shrugged. "You can't blame a girl for safeguarding her assets. Where money is concerned, some men might be tempted to take advantage of the situation." She paused to eat another truffle, the rich caramel center salty and sweet. "No children then?"

He had never mentioned any and she had never asked.

Christian's brows drew down. "No, but Sandy had wanted children. We had discussed it at length, but I wasn't so sure having kids was the right thing for us."

Was there a hint of regret in his voice? Sorrow?

"What do you have against children?"

He flashed a rakish grin. "Kids require too much attention. Not to mention the expenses associated with raising them." He paused, a look of resignation in his eyes. "I wasn't ready for that, you see. Too selfish—always have been. I wanted to travel the world with Sandy, just the two of us, without childcare concerns." He drained his glass and refilled it, staring off again. "As it was, we could have gone anywhere, done anything. The sky was the limit."

"True," Minerva said. "And then she died."

Christian glared at Minerva. "Yes." Why did she harp on Sandy's death? He quaffed his bourbon, then stood, slapped his wadded napkin onto his empty plate, and snatched up the envelope. "Come on."

A hint of a smile lifted one corner of Minerva's mouth as she stroked the stem of her champagne flute, her lavender gaze hypnotic. "Where are we going?"

"I need some air."

"Sounds like a plan."

She followed him to the aft cockpit, where he scrambled to unfold two deck chairs. He motioned to one and she sat down while he plopped into the other. He glanced at the envelope in his hand, then at her. Was he doing the right thing? He'd never done anything this crazy. What he was about to give her cost more than Sandy's extravagant, one-of-a-kind engagement ring. Way more. Was Minerva worth it? She messed with his head, scuttled his mind, left him feeling unbalanced, out of control, and the situation intensified with each encounter.

Maybe she was a witch.

Hell, might as well give it to her now.

Christian cleared his throat. "Day and night, you dominate my thoughts." He paused for a ragged breath in an attempt to steady his voice. "Try as I might, I can't get you out of my head. I daresay you have a stronger hold on me than Sandy did."

He presented the envelope. Witnessed by the moon and stars, Minerva received it from his shaking hand, removed the card and the folded paper inside. When she finished reading, she looked at him, one sculpted brow raised.

"You are giving me this yacht?"

Christian nodded, incapable of speech.

Minerva's seductive smile inflamed her eyes. "I'm flattered you hold me in such high regard. *Spiritsong* will make a fine addition to my fleet."

Then she was on her feet and so was he, the envelope and its contents abandoned in her chair. She ground her lithe body against him, stoking his desire, and cradled his face between gentle hands as she fixed him with those compelling lavender eyes. They glowed, twin moons in her ethereal face, reflecting the light of the Harvest Moon above. In the space of a single heartbeat, he lost his bearings, drowning in their depths.

Her lips claimed his, hungry and primal.

Insatiable.

It was all he could do to breathe.

"Let go." Minerva murmured the words into his open mouth. "Hold nothing back."

Christian surrendered his will under the influence of her sensuous voice. Her words were a melody in his mind, their haunting strains turning his knees to jelly. He staggered in her embrace but managed to remain upright. Blood rushed through his ears in roaring waves echoing the desperate beat of his heart as he clung to Minerva, her slender form a lifeline in the encroaching darkness.

He was doomed.

"Finish your tale about Sandy," Minerva whispered, her lips a breath from Christian's ear. "How did she die?" She kissed him, teasing his bottom lip with her tongue. "Tell me how she died, and I promise not to speak of it further. The truth shall set you free."

"Sh-she fell and b-broke her neck." Christian jerked. "It was an accident. She was helping me secure the dinghy after a late-night excursion. I lost control of the d-davit, knocking her off balance. Sandy fell and landed in the cockpit. She was dead by the time I got to her. According to the coroner, she broke her neck."

"But there is more to the story."

"No." He shook his head, his tone desperate. "What are you talking about?"

"Oh, darling Chris, surely you know what I'm talking about. Perhaps a refreshing swim will jog your memory." Maintaining eye contact, Minerva removed her cherished necklace and placed it on her chair, then withdrew through the transom door to the swim platform, beckoning with a crooked finger. "What are you waiting for?"

Then she dove into the lake.

When Minerva surfaced, Christian stood on the swim plat-form, shirtless and barefoot, arms dangling at his sides. She flicked water at him with her wide iridescent tail fin, the silver scales covering the lower half of her body shimmering like diamonds in the moonlight. Her body tingled with the magic of transformation.

"You're a m-mermaid?" Eyes bulging, mouth agape, Chris-tian shoved both hands through his hair. "I-I knew it. I knew there was something *different* about you."

"The world is full of wonders, darling Chris. Now hurry up and join me. Don't you want to reap the benefits of this precious liquid luxury?" She held water aloft in her cupped hands, then released it. "Oh, by the way, thank you for your generous gift. If I ever need an infusion of cash, *Spiritsong* will fetch a nice sum from the right buyer."

Before Christian could respond, Minerva began to sing. Spellbound by the power of her song, he leapt and swam toward her, straight into her awaiting arms.

"You pushed the dinghy into Sandy, causing her to fall. One of my associates saw what happened that night while watching from the shadows. If only I had known about it sooner..."

Smiling, Minerva pulled him underwater and unleashed her song. With her sensitive hearing, she detected the sound of Christian's heart pounding in his chest, a staccato accompani-ment to her mournful melody. She squeezed him and he struggled with the need to breathe. Just before he ran out of air, she resurfaced, laughing as he coughed and spluttered.

She narrowed her eyes. "You did it on purpose, didn't you?"

"Y-yes," he gasped. Defeated, he hung limp in her arms.

"She was pregnant, too."

"Y-yes. I'm so s-sorry."

She kissed the hot tears he shed. To his credit, they were sincere, unlike his feelings of remorse. Oh, he was sorry for getting caught, no doubt, but not for what he had done. He was afraid, however. She knew the look well. His entire body shook with the fear reflected in his eyes.

"W-was she l-like you? Sh-she loved the w-water."

Minerva caught his trembling lower lip between her teeth and nipped it. "Yes, but she kept that side of her life private. Many of my kind detest humans, so secrecy ensures survival. I am sorry, darling Chris." She kissed him, hard. "You made me care for you in spite of your deed, and I shall treasure your memory. Now you must pay for your treachery."

She slipped beneath the undulating surface of the lake, Christian in tow, the Harvest Moon's silver spears of light casting an ominous glow in the murky depths. Releasing him, she began to sing and extended her hand, descending lower with each movement of her tail. Heedless of the danger, he followed her, bulbous eyes focused on her face, unable to turn back, lured downward by her inescapable siren-song, trailing bubbles as he sank.

Time to find the perfect shell.

The End

ABOUT CRYSTAL

Crystal Lee writes fantasy stories celebrating love and the extraordinary elements of life. When not reading and writing, she watches DVDs with her errant Muse and enjoys the flowers in her secret garden. She lives in the country with her beloved Dark Knight and their feline extraordinaire, Shadow. Visit her web-haven to learn more: www.crystalrlee.com.

RED CLAY BLUES

TOM WINSTEAD

I guess it's a good thing that I can recognize my depression. I think Lily can recognize it, too—she is always quick with a smile for me, since her mother passed on. Died. Jesus, I hate the euphemisms.

Like her mother, she's a spirited little soul—an old one. Loves music. Saxophones in particular. Can tell the difference between Bird and Coltrane and Lester Young at the age of ten. Her mother said it ran in the family—that there was an uncle 'Redbone' Clay that traveled the south and the Atlantic seaboard from New Orleans to New York City, but he never made it big, never recorded an album. I never even met the dude.

Uncle Red would be about 64 or 65 years old now, I think, and Lily was sure we'd find him playing in a band one day. It had become our thing—outdoor concerts and festivals within a few hours' drive from home—just about any kind of music. And that's how we found ourselves in Florence, Alabama, at the W.C. Handy music festival on a steamy July Saturday. Lily listened to live music as one much older might worship. It seemed to make her glow with something more than just happiness. Serenity. Otherworldliness.

We had been to the college campus stages all morning at UNA, and the afternoon was wearing on. She wanted to go to the big stage located outside the Alabama Music Hall of Fame. She had overheard somebody talking about an All-Star jazz band playing that evening.

I wasn't relishing the idea of a hot July night, sweltering with a crowd, all the noise, and the smell of funnel cakes and cotton candy. But I knew it was my depression. I have tried to learn to say yes. Not to everything, just to everything within my power, especially where my precious Lily was concerned.

We stepped off of the shuttle and moved slowly through the gates in that bovine way that festival crowds move. Lily looked up at me and grinned when she sensed my frustration with the pace. "Moo, Papa!"

"Moo to you too!" I said, faking a smile. She squeezed my hand. "It's going to be okay, Papa. Can't you hear the saxophones?"

I picked her up and whispered "moo" in her ear, and kissed her on the cheek. She giggled and I set her down as we made our way onto the hay-strewn concourse of the festival. Half redneck county fair, half rock-concert. She pulled me toward the nearest tent to listen to some very energetic gospel music.

Madame Devlin sat at a small round table, dressed in the summer heat like a carnival gypsy in layered shawls and a long gown, her hands outstretched on either side of a perfect crystal ball, gently holding the hands of a strawberry blonde teenage girl, not quite eighteen. The girl was on the verge of tears.

She silently thanked God in heaven for air conditioning, and the cool air in the velveteen tent that she schlepped from fair to concert venue to art show.

"You will have the child." Madame Devlin whispered. Her real name was Leah Jones, and she'd inherited the gypsy schtick and the fake name from her grandmother, a Hungarian woman who had emigrated to a Caribbean isle as a teenager. It afforded her a decent living, and she only had to work a few days a week. She got to travel and see the south that she loved. She got to avoid too many *entanglements*. People always wore out their welcome way too soon for her liking.

She affected dark, heavy makeup which made her caramel skin look a few shades darker than her Romani/Caribe heritage accounted for. She painted on red lips and wore onyx black hair, courtesy of a very old wig. All of it made her look much older than her hard-won 34 years. She looked very much like a stereotypical side-show seer, or a voodoo queen off the streets of New Orleans. In fact, she was a touch of both.

Her grandmother had told her that the wig was made of human hair from a real Hungarian gypsy. Leah had been horrified to learn this, but leaned into it—that was Grandma's way—and she now felt as comfortable in the getup as in her own hair, her own jeans and t-shirts.

The little blonde started sobbing in earnest, and squeezed Leah's hands more firmly. "W...w...will he marry me?"

Leah—Madame Devlin—peered into the crystal ball. She saw a swirl of colors, and they spiraled down from a neutral greenish blue into a dark red. She knew what that meant. She saw this young girl standing alone with a little boy. "No. He will not."

The girl sobbed and shook, silently.

"But..."

"But what?" she asked, wiping her face with the sleeve of her shirt, and rubbing her hands together.

"But it's a good thing. He is not."

"I know."

"Good child...do not worry."

The girl bolted upright and stepped toward the door, still wiping tears from her eyes. "Thank you, Madame Devlin."

Leah raked the money off of the table into a pocket sewn into her shawl.

He wandered aimlessly around the fairgrounds, a well-worn but well-kept Selmer Paris tenor saxophone strapped around his neck. It hung there like a natural appendage, and rested against his body without effort. He stood at the side of the main stage, where a frenetic southern roots-rock trio hashed out some originals that sounded like any number of bands from the region.

They were young white guys—probably college students from UNA—and they were good. Red just didn't think they were good enough. So many musicians strove for competence and quit growing there. That's what these guys were—competent. Not special. The worst of it was they sounded like someone else. Red edged away from the stage, toward one of the side concourses, and saw a little tent. Something about it intrigued him, even though he knew that fortune tellers were usually full of shit.

As he approached the tent, he saw the previous customer wiping tears from her eyes and shielding them from the sun. *Looks like a good one*, he thought. Might have some fun. He ducked into the opening and stepped into the cool, dim light inside.

Leah looked up and gasped, then just stared at the man who had entered her tent. He had a faintly visible aura around him, a dim white and purple halo around his entire body, including the instrument strapped to his neck. The man smiled at her, almost laughing at her reaction to him.

"I'm sorry," she said. "I think you just startled me."

"You open for business, or should I go?" the man said. He raked one thumb toward the exit. His deep baritone voice filled the tent, but not harshly. His voice was like a warm hug, and his face was a human question mark. "How 'bout you tell me what for?" He started aimlessly digging through his pockets for money.

Leah quickly patted the table just beside the crystal ball. "Have a seat. No charge." She didn't know why she had offered a free reading. *THAT* had never happened before, and it wasn't like she could afford to be too generous.

"Okay then." Red sat opposite Leah and turned the saxophone to his side, letting it rest along the side of the chair and his right thigh. He removed the damp reed from his mouth and slid it into his shirt pocket.

Leah looked at the man, then into the crystal in front of her. Grandma always said, don't give it any ideas. Don't think into it. She couldn't tell if it was from her, or the man sitting across from her, but she felt a bit of dizziness, and then started to swoon to the point that she had to hold the edges of the table to keep from falling. It was happening again. It had been so long that she had forgotten to believe in her gift of sight. For the most part, she thought, it was a parlor trick. But this felt different. It felt real.

Redbone Clay cleared his throat. "How do we proceed? What do you need from me?"

Leah laughed nervously, and said, "Let me just see what I can see. If you get uncomfortable, just say 'no more'. Give me your hands."

Red lay his hands on either side of the crystal ball. Leah gently caressed his weathered brown hands with hers. "Look into the glass with me, and listen to me for a while."

He chuckled, and did as he was told. Leah looked at the inverted reflection of the man's face, and began to speak.

"You have the gift of light and sound. Rare is the gift you have, and it defines you. You are unaware. It makes no difference the voice you use," she nodded at the saxophone. "You live and die the vibrations; you are on the inside. All things are frequencies you can see or hear—color and sound—but there are frequencies that only you can feel. You have transcended one and all, you feel one and all. Your blood is here, and it is searching—but it will never see you, only hear you, because you are on the wrong side..."

Leah's head drooped, and she jerked upright as if awaking. "Do you want to get started?"

Red stared at her with his mouth wide, his eyes squinting. "Wait. What, what does that mean? I just wanted to know if anyone would hear me play? Why can't I get a gig?"

Leah looked at the crystal ball, and then her hands, and began to shake softly. She knew something was wrong, but did not know if she had truly spoken the words that had come into her mind. She stood, her arms hanging limp. "I'm sorry Mister, but you've gotta go."

———

Lily dragged me from stage to stage. We heard great blues, some really bad hip-hop, and some more passable southern rock.

We got that mid-afternoon kind of tired and hungry, so I bought us a couple of corndogs and a couple of bottles of ice-

45

cold water. Lily ate about half of her dog and gave the rest to me, but she finished her water and most of mine. She had a little curl of mustard on her lip. I wiped it off and kissed her cheek. My little angel.

"I hope the All-Star band is good! I want to hear some really great saxes and trumpets and even trombones!!"

"You will sweetie. You're not gonna get sleepy on me, are you?" We had about an hour's drive home, back to the east to Huntsville. It was always the darkest drive, even in the full moonlight, and it made me sleepy just thinking about it. Sometimes you drove right into a full moon, a train racing beside you, separated by dark trees and skies serrated by high and ghostly clouds.

She stomped her feet and said, "No, Papa! This is it! We'll find him! He's here I can feel it!"

"What are you talking about?" I tried to give her my best *'you're crazy'* look, but I knew what, and who, she was talking about.

She folded her arms in defiance and looked sideways at me. "I promise, Papa, I won't get tired." For a second, she looked just like her mother. The freckles on her face looked like a beautiful galaxy of stars.

Red walked out of the tent chuckling. He pulled the reed from his pocket and put it between his lips, moistening the thin piece of bamboo so it'd be ready to play at a moment's notice.

"Hey, what's your name?" The seer had followed him out of the tent, and seemed a little off. But the whole day had been a little off.

"My name's Red. Redbone Clay."

"I'm Leah. Madame Devlin. I'm not really sure what just

happened in there." She reached out to shake his hand, but he kept his at his sides.

Red could see a whisper of sweat on the woman's upper lip, and a bit more on her forehead. In the light of day, he could tell that her black hair was a wig. She had beautiful skin and an understated beauty about her. If not beauty, it was reality. She was real. He liked that. Most of the people he met these days were not.

"I'm not sure what happened. All that stuff you said didn't make much sense, except for the vibrations and all. I am, as you can see, a musician." Red gestured the length of his saxophone.

"I didn't really say anything, but I need to right now. You'll find him by the big stage around 7pm. That's all I really know, and I don't know what it means."

With that, the strange woman dropped to the ground like a bag of rocks. Several bystanders rushed to her, and Red turned around and took his leave, weaving through the crowd like a ghost. *Shit's getting weird around here.*

Lily led me around by the hand, and we finally found a place to sit in the shade for a while near enough the front of the main stage. The Taylor-Chambers Project was on the main stage now, playing jazz standards and originals that were informed by old jazz, new jazz, and modern pop. Excellent musicians all, it made me feel like the day had not been a waste.

Lily ate it up. She loved the way the trumpet and vocals worked seamlessly and respectfully of one another, and was entranced with the tall slim woman commanding the center of the stage. I don't know what was more beautiful, this woman singing, or her voice.

I looked at Lily and she appeared to be totally inside the music. And a carbon copy of her mother.

It had only been two years, but it seemed like yesterday. I still had an emptiness in my core that I felt every single day, and so many questions. *Why,* mostly. And Lily seemed to understand it all, and hurt less than me. I didn't know if it was her old-soul maturity, or just little-girl obliviousness. Probably a touch of both.

"Papa, don't do that. Listen." She squeezed my arm and snuggled against me, sighing and taking in the music.

"I'm sorry, sweetie. You know me."

"Papa, you have to believe me. Momma's okay. She's in the music. Just listen and you'll see her."

"I believe you. I truly do." And I listened. But I didn't have my little girl's gift of sight. Didn't have her ears. All I had was that hole in my heart.

Red hovered around the side of the main stage. No one bothered him because of the saxophone, he guessed. He found a stack of pallets to sit on, keeping him off of the hay and the red Alabama dirt. He pondered his life, which he felt like was all he ever did. Seemed like it had taken forever to live. The 'Madame' hadn't helped. She spewed gibberish that sounded sane and insane at the same time. Told me I'd meet 'him' here. *Him who?*

The side of the stage was bustling with activity as the stage hands and musicians broke down the previous act, and started setting up big-band style music stands, with the "Alabama All-Star Band" logo, adorned with glittered stars and flames. The glitter was old and barely sparkled. This looked like a 'vintage' act, but most of the musicians milling around and setting up looked to be in their twenties.

"Clarence! Is that you?" An elderly black man in a pristine vintage 1920's suit walked up to Red. The lapels were piped, and the vest had a golden paisley pattern to it. He wore a black bow-tie that looked brand new. The man was resplendent, if not 80 or 90 years of age.

"Excuse me?" The man looked familiar. He had that quality about him that is unmistakable in people of wide fame. But Red couldn't place him. He thought he knew everybody in the business. "I'm sorry I…"

"No worries, my man—you're not late. I just wanted to go over a couple of changes." The old man grasped his right hand and shook it heartily. "It is so good to see you. It feels like a hundred years!" He held a raw brass cornet in his left hand. Something about him…

Red smiled, and did his best to pretend to know what the hell was happening. This is the man the seer was talking about. He got that much.

Someone behind the main stage shouted "William!" The older man turned, and said, "Be right back. Just one thing, you go first on the solos. Urb will go second, and then me. Just wanted to do it the old way."

"Okay…"

But the old man was already on a beeline to the back of the stage.

Leah woke up on the floor of her tent, and wondered how she had gotten there. She sat up and took inventory. The vague purple hues in the tent calmed her.

She found nor felt any damage, except that her hip was a little sore, and her wig was slightly askew. She got to one knee and lifted herself up by the edge of the table, dropping heavily into the chair on the customer's side of the table.

As she settled, the clear orb on the table wobbled in its black marble base, settling heavily into the round onyx cradle that her grandmother had said was crafted from a large chunk of meteorite. She never quite knew what was bullshit, and what wasn't, where her grandmother was concerned. As a child she had believed everything—but in retrospect, it seemed made-up. Maybe it wasn't the Real. Maybe it never was.

Never was. The Real. Stuff her grandmother used to say all the time.

She looked into the crystal and saw the old man with a bow-tie, glowing orange eyes, and a malevolent grin. She quickly folded the table-cloth over the orb and whispered "Quiet..."

She heard someone stepping into the tent, and without turning to face them, Leah said, "I'm closing up for the day."

A woman's heavy, Alabama accented voice, said, "I just wanted to make sure you are okay, sweetie. You took quite a spill. Me and Earl dragged you back in here. You seemed to be breathing okay. Do you want us to call somebody?"

Leah turned to the woman, who looked much younger than her voice. "No, thank you. I'm fine. Did you see the man with the saxophone? The one I was talking to?"

The woman smiled. "I didn't see nobody with no saxophone. I just saw you hit the ground. Are you sure you okay?"

Leah nodded and stood up, facing the woman. "Thank you. Thank you so much." She leaned in for a hug and the woman reciprocated, then turned and ducked out of the tent.

An older gentleman in a vintage suit stepped into the space the woman had vacated, with a grace Leah felt she was imagining.

"Sorry to bother, miss...Devlin?"

Leah stood straight upright. The man seemed so familiar, but she couldn't place him. Until his eyes began to glow a dark amber light.

"What do you want?" she said.

"You know."

He handed her his ancient cornet. It felt heavy, and altogether unreal to her. Warmer than it should have been. Hard metal to the touch, but not the cold she would have expected.

He stepped closer to her, and placed his right palm on her forehead. His hand felt warm, and Leah realized that she could not recoil, couldn't even blink. He smiled at her, but it was not a friendly smile. Leah's entire being was screaming in panic, but she could not move, and couldn't make a sound.

The old man picked up the orb on the table, held it up to his eyes, and smiled. He dropped it into his leather satchel, a man's messenger bag, then turned and wrested his horn from her grasp. He stood and straightened his bow-tie, and exited the tent as silently as he had entered.

Leah stood motionless until she realized she was shaking. Tears ran from both of her eyes. *Have I just seen the devil?*

<hr>

The All-Star Band was SMOKING! Lily sat in rapt attention as the band went through songs that were at least 80 years old, but the sound was new. She looked at me, and I saw the light in her eyes. She smiled and held onto my arm. It was absolute heaven.

The saxophone player took his solo and Lily got so excited I thought she might burst. Then the trombonist, who wove an entirely unexpected melody over the familiar song—I think it was "Do Nothing Til You Hear From Me," played at a thundering clip. Then the trumpet player took center stage.

The band was set up saxes, then trombones, then trumpets, rows of 5—4—and 4 to the right of the stage, with the drums to the left of the horns, a cacophonic barrier between the piano and upright bass. The old man with the small trumpet strode forward amid the huge music machine. His solo was devastating.

"It's a cornet, Papa, not a trumpet." Lily whispered. I shuddered, but at the time, didn't wonder how she read my mind. All that came later.

I've never heard anything in my life like his solo. I saw Eddie Van Halen once. I saw Tab Benoit and Stevie Ray Vaughn. You expect this kind of power and magic from a great guitarist with a giant bank of amplifiers behind them. But not from a trumpet. Sorry. A cornet. It brought the heavens down.

———

Red felt like he had died and gone to heaven. The band was on it! Everything was like it should have been. They played effortlessly through a set for the ages, every song a triumph of arrangement, execution, and individual excellence. He couldn't remember ever having played so well. William grinned at him through the solos, and they reached their final tune. Red took his solo, and brought tears to his own eyes. He had never done that. Urb smoked through his trombone solo.

Then came William.

Somebody in the band shouted "W.C. Mothereffer..."

Holy shit. Red felt like he had been struck by lightning as the history of music, hundreds of years, the birth of jazz in America, all of those things hit him at the same time, and he knew. *This cannot be.*

The man with the cornet and the satchel at his feet played like a demon. There was no one within earshot who was not staring at the man, even as he began to glow in the stage lights. Amber, orange, red, and even black—the lights of the world we all fear. But none could look away.

———

Thunder cracked. The crowd gasped as one. It had been a hot day with high cumulus clouds and heavy humidity, but nothing had hinted at rain, and none had been forecast. The day had fallen to darkness while we were all distracted.

Lightning blazed across the backdrop of the stage, and large rain drops started pelting down, building quickly to a steady pour. Everyone jumped from their chairs and seats and blankets, and started making their way for the exits. I looked at the stage, and it had been quickly abandoned by musicians and crew alike. It seemed like a magic trick on a monumental scale. Lily took my hand. "Come on Papa!"

She pulled me toward the Alabama Music Hall of Fame building, instead of the direction that the majority of the crowd had decided to go.

We made it to a side door which was open wide with a few staffers and stragglers making their way in. The door, once opened, wasn't to be closed until we all made it in, safe from the rain and thunder.

It was a respite from hell, in retrospect. Compared to the heat of the day, the building was frigid, but what hit me the most was how dry the air seemed on such a humid day. It almost hurt to breathe the brittle air. Lily continued to lead me by the hand, and we stumbled past the exhibits.

We made it to a bench beside the W.C. Handy section of the Hall. Pictures and instruments and photos lined the L-shaped free-standing walls. The man in the pictures looked eerily like the man playing the cornet, though much younger. I turned to Lily, seated beside me on the bench, and she was breathing heavily. "Are you all right, sweetie?"

She took my hand and said, "I told you we'd find him. It's all going to be okay. Let me do this."

I looked up and the man was standing less than ten feet away, cornet in hand, a rain-pelted leather satchel over his shoulder. He looked at the display with a wide, nearly maniacal smile, and began to laugh. The saxophone player stumbled into the Hall behind him, followed by a woman who looked like a gypsy. I remember it all. But what I remember most of all, is that I couldn't move. I was frozen in something between time and space, as were the other people in the hall. Lily stood and walked toward the old man, and he hissed at her. "What do you want, little girl?"

Leah stumbled toward Red as if in a daze. "We have to stop him."

Red slumped as if he finally understood what was happening. "Every time I have a decent gig..."

Lily walked to the fortune teller and took her hand. She spoke with innocence as she pulled her away from Red, but turned to him with a huge smile. "Hi, Uncle Red! You played great. Just like Momma said you would!" Red smiled and looked at the little girl, whose eyes glowed with a white ethereal light. She pulled the fortune teller toward the man called William.

"Mr. Handy, if that is who you chose to be in this ain't, you need to return a few items."

He leaned down and looked directly into Lily's eyes. "No. Not this time. This is MY time."

"No. Your time is long past. Long stored. A story long told. Over." She held out her hand. "Give them both to me. My Momma's, and Miss Devlin's. They are not yours. What you are trying to do will not work. It never works."

William screamed. "I WILL NOT."

Lily held out her hand and remained calm. Nothing about this seemed to be strange to her. In my state I could not feel fear, only cold. I could not move—this man, this thing stood and screamed and gestured nothing but threat to my little girl, and I could not move.

The old man reached into the bag, scowling such hate as I've never seen. "Here." He placed a large crystal ball into my daughter's hands. She took it and handed it to the seer.

"The other one."

"But that one's MINE!"

"It is. But it is not yours to own, or to keep. You belong in it. It is your time—your story. But the story is over."

The man began to cry. "Please..."

Lily reached and took his free hand gently. "I know. But you have to understand. To transcend is possible, but not for you. The math doesn't work yet."

"But it will!"

"Give it to me."

The man reached into his satchel and brought out an identical crystal ball. Lily took it effortlessly, and held it between them. She regarded the old man. "Don't be afraid."

"I was great! I don't deserve this!"

"No. You got that wrong. You ARE great. And 'deserve' is not an infinite concept. Be who you are. Were."

She stared into the crystal, her eyes that ethereal violet/purple/white that I had seen so often, but much brighter, much more intense. The orb began to glow, and I tried to close my eyes but I couldn't. She held it up to the man's forehead. The cornet player, the band leader, the writer and musician, turned into orange/red light and got sucked—instrument and all—into the sphere. He vanished in a mere moment.

I tried to look around, but I still couldn't move. The people around us were as frozen as I. Only Lily, the gypsy, and Uncle Red seemed normal. Normal? Is that a word I'll ever use again?

Lily turned to Leah. "Hold onto your crystal ball with everything you've got."

The woman looked deeply confused, deeply worried, but she complied none-the-less.

Lily took the ball that had just absorbed a grown man, and pressed it against the one the gypsy held. The lights were so bright this time I feared that if I could not close my eyes, I would lose my sight. But I couldn't. Couldn't shield them with my hands. It was like looking at the sun, or a weld in progress, it hurt and burned and shook the building, my heart, and my very soul.

The ball that Lily held was absorbed by the one that Miss Devlin held, until they were one.

Lily took the single remaining ball from her and turned to the saxophone player.

"I'm very proud of you. I have always wanted to hear you play!"

Red smiled and knelt down, looking at eye level with my little girl. "I've always wanted to meet you too. I don't know what is happening."

Lily beamed at him. "My momma always bragged on you. You were always a big deal in our family."

Red's head dropped and he began to sob, but he caught himself, and looked back into Lily's eyes. "That's the nicest thing I've ever heard."

"This won't hurt, Uncle Red. It'll actually be good. You'll be where you belong, and you'll never have another day without a gig."

"Oh darlin', I'm ready for that. *Ti Bon Ange*." It was what she had always called Lily. *Ti Bon Ange*—her little good angel.

Lily held the orb to Red's forehead, and the world exploded.

I stood up and saw the people filing out of the Hall. The rain had stopped and the security guards were asking everyone to make their way to the exits. Lily was giving the crystal ball back to the woman. Everything seemed like a dream.

"Thank you."

Lily regarded her solemnly. "Take special care of this. It's important."

"I get it. I know that now. Are they in the same place now?"

Lily shook her head slowly, "No, they're each in their own places. William can't hurt Red anymore. They weren't meant to be there together anyway. It's all good."

She sighed. "What am I supposed to do?"

Lily grinned. "Be you! Keep doing what you do! Do it with love, and do it for real."

The woman knelt down and hugged Lily. Then she walked toward the exits with the remnants of the crowd.

Lily took my hand. We looked at the display, all of the W.C. Handy artifacts, pictures, and the glass case with his old cornet. Painted in script along the side of the display were Alabama musicians that somehow rated an honorable mention: Keith Chambers, Greg Taylor, Dave Watters, Kenny Anderson, and Clarence "Redbone" Clay, about whom they say Freddie Hubbard penned the jazz standard "Red Clay."

She led me to the shuttle, and we made our way back to the car.

I don't remember the drive home.

Leah drove her small Ford van south into Mississippi on the Natchez Trace Parkway. Her tent, furniture, and all of her clothing were stowed tightly in the back. Her crystal ball was in an old leather bowling-ball case right behind the empty passenger seat. It was a slower route, and she'd have to get onto bigger highways in time, but it would serve her purpose.

She needed to think.

She didn't really know what it was she had witnessed, but it had meant two human beings leaving our plane and entering her crystal ball. No—not right. One entered another ball, then that ball entered hers, then the nice man entered hers. And really, were they human?

She thought about the little girl. Red had called her '*ti bon ange*'—Little Good Angel. A chill ran down her spine.

She wondered—did that really mean they were separated? What could it possibly be? How much is in there? How many of those crystal balls are there? *And she knew without knowing, that there is not a word for a number big enough. 'Infinite' doesn't really even do it justice.*

She drove, sipped on a small bottle of mineral water, and listened to the music inside her head.

Man, Alabama is always such a trip.

Can't wait to get home to New Orleans, where everything is normal.

The End

ABOUT TOM

Tom Winstead is a writer, musician, and luthier. A bassist from an early age, Tom began building basses in 2017, creating the brand Redstone Bass Guitars. He published his first work of fiction, "Seven Steps to Heaven" in The Silver Web in 1996. Seven Steps received both Nebula and Hugo nominations, and received an honorable mention in Ellen Datlow's Year's Best Science Fiction and Fantasy. Tom has had 30+ short stories, reviews, and opinion pieces published in SF and Fantasy small press outlets. He lives in Huntsville, AL where he is a working bassist, author, and builder.

POPPET

LESLIE SCOTT

A Black Water Magic Short Story

Samhain, for a witch, was a really big deal. And it brought more jitters than I had on my first day of high school—complete with random magical outbursts. I was working on that.

Other witches from all over Florida were coming to my neighbor Shelley's backyard brouhaha. I'd helped with the decorations around the Crazy Eight trailer park all week—more harvest-like and less commercial. Except, I was pretty sure the bones, hidden here and there, were real.

And since I got to stay home from school, I'd helped Teagan Blackwater, the resident Swamp Witch of Firewater Springs add witch-lights to lanterns. When we finished, she'd left me with Shelley to hang them in her fenced backyard. Which *looked* like it wasn't much bigger than a parking space.

But it was huge, complete with a garden and stone greenhouse. I always felt like I'd been transported to a different time —a different world.

Every witch is different. The way magic is wielded is unique to each person. Sort of like how no two voices really sound the same. And Shelley's particular affinity was making things, potions and the like, and it was my turn to help her. A home-grown magic, not necessarily battle magic—Oliver, my mentor, called her a garden witch. One time I watched her dispose of demon fledglings with a garden hose and a weedkiller attachment.

I still hadn't found what made me cool, or different. Unless you counted the pink goat thing—I hadn't seen anyone make a goat. I wish I could figure out what made me special, maybe then I wouldn't be invisible to pretty much everyone in existence.

The crack of two fingers snapping together jerked my chin around. Shelley McAllister waved her hand in my face. "Hello, Anna, you in there?"

"Yeah." I blinked a few times and focused on the assortment of colored bottles and jars that glinted in front of me. Some were so old the glass had yellowed so I couldn't see what was inside. Others were bright and vibrant. And still others were caked in dirt, as if they'd been long buried.

"This is important stuff. You can't always pour energy into spells, wards, and other protections. Jars and bottles are a good way to keep yourself safe—you store the magic in them, it feeds off itself, and the spell is continuously armed."

Shelley's special magic was all of this sort of stuff. She was like a magical MacGyver. Oliver thought I needed to learn this sort of stuff too. *Yay. Great.* But it beat reading another long ass book about malevolent entities or energies or whatever my homework had been last week.

If I couldn't be vibing out to some music and turning demon spawn into livestock, at least this was *something*. It had been months since we'd vanquished a carnival of demi-demons, and I was still riding what Oliver had called the battle high.

The excitement of my first Halloween as a witch was enough to keep my eyes from crossing as Shelley droned on about different things to put in the jars to capture different types of magic. The rusty nails in one bottle, were a nice touch. When I held it up, Shelley continued. "This one is planted near the northwest corner of your home. The nails are to impale evil spirits."

"Don't wards protect against that sort of thing?" The entirety of the Crazy Eight Mobile Home Park was encased in a megawatt magical forcefield.

"You won't find leylines or the magic they present everywhere you go, Anna."

Having never lived anywhere else, it was hard to imagine not having the current of magic that surrounded Firewater Springs, Florida.

"The jar is a self-sustaining spell. You can use a jar anywhere, for any purpose, and not have to constantly charge it.

"There are all sorts of ways to make jars and bottles, with a variety of uses." Shelley blew a tuft of blond hair from her face. "Like that smoky blue one."

I picked up the bottle she'd gestured at. The blue glass was coated in a fog that didn't allow me to see the contents.

"Give it a shake."

As soon as I did, the damn thing let out a wailing shriek so sharp I almost dropped it. Shelley's face lit up, amused. "Residual banshee energy."

"Those things are real?" I placed the bottle down with as much ease as my trembling arm could muster and checked the cork to make sure it was still firmly in place. I'd read some of that book Oliver had given me, and banshees seemed downright terrifying.

"Sort of, yeah. I think." She shrugged. "Energy, though, exists. Sometimes so dense, it takes on a life of its own." She moved the banshee bottle over by several others. "Some of that energy causes problems, some doesn't. The harmless sprites— living manifestations of energy—pass through the bottles unharmed and become part of the power you feel all around us. The rest? Go in the jars."

"Weird." And maybe a little mean, when I thought about it. "What about these?" Three squat, fat jars caked in mud resided at the corner of the table. They looked like they'd been buried for decades.

Shelley sighed, picked one up, and rolled it between her fingers. "Hex jars. I made them for my ex. But he'll be here tonight to take the boys trick or treating. With these here, he couldn't—so I'll have to destroy them."

If Shelley had gone that far to keep him away, there had to be a reason. I shivered. "Will you be okay?"

"Yeah." With a snort, she added things to a jar before handing the job off to me. "I'm not afraid of him, never was. When I felt like he didn't have any business in my personal space anymore, I cast him out."

Shelley treated me like a peer. She talked to me, not at me.

Under the cauldron in the middle of the greenhouse, she built a small fire. Then she sprinkled something from a tiny glass vial into the large, iron bowl. White flame burst from within, reaching to the ceiling but burning nothing.

"If the jars aren't destroyed properly, it could harm the witch that made them."

I raised a brow, as she whispered something against a jar before smashing it into the white flames. They sizzled and danced, and the scent of something fragrant rushed through the room.

She repeated the process two more times. "I had to make a point, that we were finished." Her voice was filled with a quiet strength.

"And now?" I was intrigued, as Shelley had never even mentioned the boys' father to me before. She had two small children and often dropped them off for visits. But otherwise rocked that single mom vibe.

The look on her face was sort of wistful and sad. "Now, it doesn't matter so much—it's about the boys. This is the first Samhain they'll sort of have a grip on what is going on."

"Are they dressing up?" This was one human tradition I hoped the witches carried on with. I freaking loved Halloween and all its customs.

"Yup." She moved back to the table and laid out several small, blue bundles of herbs and other dried plants. "Light these, then blow them out as soon as they catch fire. Cover the smoke with a jar. Move on to the next. Finish these few, while I go grab some more."

I nodded, used to Shelley leaving me to work while she disappeared into the bowels of the greenhouse to retrieve more materials. I swear, she had everything in this place. The seed vault in Norway had nothing on Shelley McAllister.

The jars containing the mischievous sprites were all different bright colors. I couldn't help but think of them as little, misunderstood fairies. I knew all about that. The older witches tried, but I wasn't the same, and they knew it.

Imagining a life spent cooped up in a jar, lacking all freedom, I picked up the purple one, turned it over in my hand and squinted past the foggy glass to the sticks and polished stones inside. No rusty nails, so maybe this guy wasn't so bad.

The glass warmed in my hands, and a sort of happy jolt rocketed up my arm. Like the energy inside was introducing itself.

"Hi there." I whispered and smiled. A kindred spirit in a jar, literally. When I moved this jar, it made a gentle tinkling sound. Maybe the spell got it wrong. Maybe this sprite was misunderstood, like me. "We could have been friends, I bet."

"What was that?" Shelley called from the back.

The jar bounced in my hands, like a kid who just got caught snooping through the internet. I bobbled it once, caught it, and bit back a laugh. Too bad I couldn't just set him free— he deserved his freedom as much as any of us.

Shelley's white flames whipped around, growing and reaching for me. Tendrils of magical flame licked at my fingers and the jar.

Then the glass disappeared. Twigs and multi-colored, polished stones scattered to the floor.

My heart dropped into the bottom of my stomach faster then I hit my knees. Teagan was going to kill me. Worse, Oliver was going to give me that super disappointed look.

Shit. Shit. Shit. The jar itself was gone completely, so I scooped the contents up and shoved them into my pocket, right as she came back.

She glanced around, stared at me curiously for just a second.

"Can't a girl tie her shoe?" I made a face like she'd lost her mind and spun away, back to my task. "I'm done with these. What's next?"

"We light the sage, blow it out so that we get good smoke, and cover it with an empty jar so that the smoke smudges the inside— cleansing it." As Shelley spoke, the jars on the table shuddered in a wave that ran from one side to the other. I laid my hand across two vibrating jars. Whatever it was, was warm and tingling and invisible, and it slid up my arm and into my hair. There, it trembled as if it were afraid—of Shelley. The least terrifying woman I'd ever met.

You should meet Teagan. The Swamp Witch had taken down a damn demon, pretty friggin scary if you asked me. The sprite gripped tightly with invisible fingers to the back of my neck. Meeting Teagan was not a good idea.

"Easy." I whispered.

"What was that?" Shelley turned to me. "Are you okay? You look pale."

I'd been nervous before. I'd lied before. What teenager didn't spit a few white lies here or there? But looking at the concern on Shelley's face made it ten times harder. I had to fix this, before it got out of hand.

I opened my mouth to tell her, but the sprite disappeared. I glanced frantically around in the several seconds before a clash of plastic and glass echoed from several lots away.

"I'm not feeling so well." I rushed past her toward the back-yard gate. "I'll be back!"

If she called after me, I didn't hear her. All the way up the street, the lids were popping off garbage cans and trash was going everywhere.

Oliver was going to kill me. That is, if the almighty Swamp Witch didn't find out about this first. I'd released a chaotic spirit, who was currently barreling through the Crazy Eight Mobile Home Park, tossing over garbage cans and upending our decorations with such force bones and wood clattered on the street.

Each time I thought I'd lost it; the mischievous thing would toss a festive yard ornament towards the road. It was like he— because it felt like a boy, a girl would be way more creative with her chaos—wanted me to find him. I knew all about doing stuff, making a mess or acting out, for attention.

My mom left when I was so little I couldn't remember her, and Dad worked sixty plus hours a week. My entire life was a series of shenanigans hoping to get someone to look at me.

"No!" My shout echoed against the Fletcher's trailer and down into the swamp. Emma and David Fletcher had spent all of the previous afternoon carving their pumpkins. I'd been there, babysitting. And now, the little sneaky thing was lifting those orange, festive decorations from the concrete patio. Both hovered and bobbled precariously a few feet from the ground.

I fought to walk slowly. If I spooked it, the sprite would toss them right onto the concrete. Splattered Jack-o-lantern guts would be bad news for my first Samhain as a witch.

"Check this out." I knelt in front of the pumpkins and as I

did, he lowered them. With deft fingers, I plucked the poppet from my pocket. "Made it with my magic. Pretty cool, huh?" I wiggled the legs around, so the small stick figure danced. Oliver had taught me how to make them. Little figures made out of weeds, threads from my clothes, and pieces of my hair.

Admittedly, I was feeling pretty stupid, crouched on the ground, talking to the magical equivalent of an imaginary friend. Talking him into what, exactly? Put down his pumpkin projectiles and play stick figure with me?

The gaping maw of one of the carved pumpkins lowered in front of me so that I was peering into it, at the remaining guts and seeds. The perspective was creepy and I fought the urge to flinch. My face was serene, my body lax, as I walked the little figure over my leg. If I freaked out, I'd spook the dang spirit and he'd be buzzing all over the neighborhood again. And I'd barely caught my breath.

Slowly he lowered the pumpkins and then a rustle slid over my arm and wrapped warmly around my hand. I slid it and the poppet into my hip pocket and stood. *Now what?* I could ask one of the older witches for help but—this would just be one more thing I'd messed up.

Fix it yourself.

The school bus pulled in just as I made it into the street. The low rumble of the diesel motor hummed along until it was interrupted by the screech of the air brakes in front of the bus stop. Neither sound seemed to affect the sprite.

The small horde of children shot out of the vehicle costumed and pumped full of sugar.

The sprite shot out of my pocket, jerking backpacks and swinging kids around, tossing one to the ground where she cried out in surprise before the waterworks came on.

When I opened my mouth to shout, afraid for the first time that he could hurt someone, something else happened. My magic.

67

The rolling wave of energy slipped over the kids and crashed into the spirit.

It tore off down the street. This time, though, I could see it. A tiny tuft of translucent purplish smoke, residue from my unintended spell clinging to it.

The sprite hovered in front of me for several seconds before bolting out of the neighborhood. At least now I could see him.

My lungs burned and my legs wiggled like rubber bands with each step by the time we reached downtown. The sprite didn't care—he zipped here and there, upending tables and carts, crashing into parked cars and shop windows, only slowing when distracted by his own reflection in a window or one lady's shining engagement ring. He nearly ripped the door off her car as she opened it.

The colorful shiny stones from the jar made perfect sense now.

I stopped, panting, as the sprite lost interest in her, darted past the car and right to the one place I avoided at all costs. Nothing glinted quite like chrome in the sunlight, and the Northman MC's Clubhouse was the perfect place to find it. He'd be in shiny thing heaven.

I stopped running, bent over my knees and gasped for breath. *Maybe dropping PE this year was a bad idea.* There was no way I was chasing him in there. Once, I'd thought the guys in the Northmen Motorcycle Club were cool and a few of them cute. But that was before my biker boyfriend had made plans to feed me to a demon.

Now I knew what the Northmen Motorcycle Club really was —a den of demi-demons. Every man in that place was a super-power-wielding half-demon, talk about some scary stuff.

Living at the Crazy Eight meant there were more reasons to

avoid trouble with the Northmen. Swamp Witch repercussions and all that, and she was the one person I couldn't afford to piss off.

I needed to get my little spirit guy out of there before he destroyed everything—including my first Samhain.

A heavy misgiving lodged itself in my stomach. I wanted to hide, barf, and maybe both. But my anxiety held me to the spot. I heard shouts and the sound of breaking glass. Here I was, the only witch within a mile, and I was right outside. *Not suspicious, not even a little bit.*

Running would draw attention, so I speed-walked down the sidewalk. Head down, staring at my toes, listening to all the commotion. The inventive and archaic cursing coming from within the clubhouse would have been hilarious any other time.

At the back of the building, the sidewalk ran out, right in front of an open door. Unlike the front of the clubhouse, the back was grassy and surrounded by thick inland Florida under-brush. Probably teeming with snakes.

Please don't go in there, little dude. I choked on the gag caught in my throat. Snakes were *not* my thing. I crouched against the brick and made one awkward attempt at blending in with the surroundings before craning my neck out to peer into the smoky chaos inside.

My sprite had gone straight for the big mirror behind the bar, knocking liquor bottles flying in every possible direction. Bikers, clad in patched leather vests, juggled the bottles to keep from dropping them and failed. Others slipped and slid on the spilled liquid. It was a big, bad, biker circus.

"What are you doing?" The voice was young and unmistak-ably male.

I peeked through my hair and jerked straight up.

He was not much older than me. Though with demi-demons and witches, apparent age could be an issue. We all aged slower, so far as I could tell. The bad part—he was cute. Like, attractive enough I had a hard time forming a coherent response to his question.

His leather vest was still new and lacked the insignia and patches of the rest, it simply read PROSPECT on his left shoulder. Not yet a Northman.

But it was the lopsided, half-flirting grin that really got my attention.

"Um, ya know..." I shrugged and tried to look impish and girl-like, twisting the hem of my shirt like I was nervous. I was, but not for the reasons I tried to portray. "I've never seen the inside of the clubhouse, and the door was open."

"Uh...huh." He tilted his head to the side. Unlike the boys at school, this dark-haired, dark-eyed cutie was tattooed. A swirling, magical symbol right under his left ear and a tribal arrow across his right forearm. I could *feel* the spell woven into the ink.

I shoved my hand in my pocket to keep from reaching for it.

"The clubhouse randomly erupts into total bedlam, and I find a witch lurking outside the back door just to take a peek?" He arched one perfect dark eyebrow and leaned down, his face right next to mine. "I ain't buying it, baby witch."

This close, he was even prettier. Smooth, blemish-free skin touched by the sun, dark whiskey-colored eyes framed by thick, dark lashes, and a crooked smile over perfect teeth. I wanted to hate him, but he was too gorgeous for that.

Whoa.

"Look, it's not my fault." In my life, I'd started way too many sentences that way. "I'm trying to fix things. I just need..."

Before I could finish, a familiar tingling of movement shot up the back of my leg and under my shirt, vibrating at the small of my back like a magical energy massager. My body almost melted in relief. The sprite was back. Now to just keep him there.

The demi-demon straightened, tilted his head ever so

slightly to the side, and crossed his arms over his chest. He knew something was up, and the lazy way he studied me made that totally obvious. My magic started to tickle at my chest, like it always did right before I did something stupid.

I reached in my pocket and wrapped my fingers around the little stick figure there, casting the energy into the poppet like I'd been taught. The thing was meant to be a magic reservoir of sorts.

A fight wouldn't get me out of this, and let's face it, there's no way I'd stand a chance against a bar full of outcast superheroes plucked from a bad graphic novel.

"Prospect!" The shout came from deep inside, and he grimaced but didn't move. "What the hell are you doing?"

The man who stuck his head out the door was squat, with a grizzled beard, and looked more like he was about to spout Dwarvish and battle dragons than use the mop he held. "Who's that?" He jabbed a pudgy finger in my direction.

"Um, this is my friend..." He relaxed his arms and cast me a look like, *well who are you?*

I hesitated long enough that he shifted from one to the other. Making a cute guy squirm was sort of fun. "Anna Bentley."

"Anna was here to find out when we'd make the delivery to the Swamp Witch's party tonight. I can drive it over now, so you don't have to later."

The squat man scowled, grunted, and shouted over his shoulder. "Want the kid to drive the drinks over to Crazy Eight?" When he turned back, he gestured with his hand. "Don't screw anything up, Eric."

Eric directed me toward a gray van at the back of the wooded area. "I can give you both a ride."

"I'm not climbing in a kidnapper van." No way. He wasn't even remotely that hot.

He chuckled. "Pretty sure that poltergeist could take me out, if you couldn't." And before I could argue, he cut me off with a look. "I've seen a thing or two. They usually attach themselves to someone and destroy their lives. Pretty crazy stuff." When I didn't respond he continued. "My mom is a clairvoyant. She keeps strange friends."

I'd spent the past hour frantically chasing after this thing while it terrorized a few blocks of Firewater Springs. If he didn't calm down...yeah, that would suck. I let disappointment settle over me like a hot, heavy thumb that was gonna press me all the way into the ground.

My first Samhain was definitely ruined. But what would the other witches do when they found out? And if this little guy was as obviously stuck to me as it felt...

Tears stung my eyes but didn't fall. I wasn't crying in front of a boy. No way.

From where it rested against my back, the little ball of energy grew angry, the heat of its emotion washing over the chill of my fear. Then he shot straight at Eric.

I'd seen a demi-demon use his powers before, and I'd used my own magic too many times to count. But I still wasn't prepared for what happened when the translucent, purple orb of energy slammed into Eric.

The sprite spun rapidly, hanging in the air right in front of the demi-demon's face. It wasn't until pieces of debris from the ground began to swirl around him, I realized the sprite was flailing about in a column of wind, caught in a mini tornado between us.

"I'm not hurting it." Eric said simply, his hands flexed out in front of him, fingers spinning slowly.

I knew he wasn't. For whatever reason, like when the sprite had been angry or scared, I could sense that he wasn't in any pain.

"I think he's having fun. That's pretty epic." My anxiety got lost in my sudden awe. "Can you, ya know, make an actual tornado?"

He sighed and cast his eyes heavenward for at least a ten count.

"Yeah, I get that a lot." I reached forward, letting a finger brush against the wind. My skin burned from the friction, and I jerked my hand back.

"Careful." He cracked that lopsided grin again and butterflies stirred in my stomach.

Uh oh. I'd accidentally turned the last guy to make me feel like that into a goat. My best bet was to stay far away from boys until I figured this whole witch thing out. That might take a few decades at this rate.

"You're going to have to convince it that I'm not going to hurt you. Otherwise, it'll keep coming for me."

"What makes you think he's going to listen to me?"

"Because it's your spirit. He's attached himself to you. You're officially haunted."

I'm not sure what I expected hauntings to be like, but this wasn't it.

"I can't keep it like this forever."

"Fine." I stopped short of stamping my foot and stepped closer to the spinning wind spirit prison. "Hey Buddy, look. Eric here, he's a good guy and is going to take us home...so we can figure out what to do with you. Okay?"

I glanced to Eric, who shrugged. "Sounds good to me."

And the tornado stopped, leaves and twigs floating back to the ground without a sound. When the sprite just hovered there, indecisively, I patted my pocket. "In you go."

Easy as anything, he flew into my pocket and stayed there trembling, and I'd imagine—dizzy. I climbed into the van, desperate to get home for help with this before things got worse. Like it or not, I was gonna have to at least tell Shelley what I'd done.

I couldn't risk the little dude hurting someone or himself. *Why me?*

"What's your plan?" Eric asked as he wheeled the van around the clubhouse. "You can't just walk around with a poltergeist in your pocket."

"No crap." I leaned back against the seat with a moan and closed my eyes. After a few seconds, I opened them and glanced at him.

Eric was cute to the point of being pretty. The errant dark curl that fell over one eye only made him better looking.

When he caught me checking him out, he offered unsolicited advice on my current predicament. Proving he wasn't as interested in me as I was in him. Thank goodness for small miracles.

"Usually, you can trap a poltergeist with what it wants. Sometimes, if you find out the thing it desires most, they go away completely." Before I could answer, he grinned again. "I don't know the why or the where, I'm not an expert. But... maybe there's something you have that he wants."

I thought about that for a long time. The sprite connected with me, not just because I'd freed it. Before that, when I held the jar, there was a similarity between us. I understood him and he understood me.

What would I want if I was causing a ruckus? I got louder, more dramatic when I wanted to be seen.

Eric pulled into the Crazy Eight and I directed him to Shelley's driveway. "What are you going to do?"

"Why do you care?" I gripped the door handle. None of this made any difference to a random demi-demon. From what I knew of his kind, they were pretty selfish creatures. The idea, that this sweet guy who bailed me out at the clubhouse was one sort of made me sick in my stomach.

"Because you seem nice, and I know what it's like, hanging out on the bottom rung of the ladder, everyone watching, thinking you're about to screw up." His honesty was visible in his earnest expression.

The idea hit me with such sudden ferocity that I was half out of the truck before I tossed my gratitude over my shoulder. "Thanks, Eric. I really appreciate it—but I've got this covered."

And all on my own, too.

The sprite seemed content in my pocket as I speed walked through the Crazy Eight toward the playground. Dad would be off work by now, so I couldn't go home. This would be entirely outside of my realm of ability to explain away.

It was close to dinner time, so the playground was empty, nobody there to notice when the sprite jolted from my pocket to weave in and out of the swings, making them sway like they were touched by the wind.

"Come on, I have something to show you." Talking to him like that was sort of weird, but he listened and followed me under the slide.

I sat in the shade quietly and closed my eyes, taking several deep breaths. Clearing my mind would help my focus, and I'd never worked a binding spell before—I'd need all the help I could get.

A sliver of broken mirror glinted in the fading sun that sneaked around the slide. I placed it and the rest of the contents from the opened jar on the ground in front of me. Then the poppet I'd been working on, using the magic I'd stored in it to cast a circle around myself.

If this went wrong, the blowback would stay in my circle and affect only me.

I can do this. My magic is strong, and I am capable. Maybe if I kept telling myself that, I could manifest it—make it true.

The sprite bounced back and forth against my circle, chasing it so far upward that I couldn't see him anymore. I couldn't tell if he was angry, but he was definitely freaking out.

"I get it, it's like a big jar." I sighed. "And I'm sorry, but this is only for a little while."

I fingered a few of the bright beads, then wove them through the twigs and string. I even managed to nestle the mirror in the middle of the poppet doll's body.

When the sprite settled down, I held up the doll. "See this guy?" The sprite moved around my hand, nudging against the bright colors and shining pieces I'd spruced the poppet up with. "I'm going to bind you to it...then you'd have a body. Everyone can see you."

There was indecision in the energy, a sort of unsure excitement that made my heart ache.

The messed up spells I'd tried to pull off had mounted into me being probably the worst witch the Crazy Eight had ever seen. None of that had ever bothered me really until now. Eric had been right, everyone was just waiting for me to screw something up so bad it couldn't be fixed.

But this was too important. I stuck the earbuds in my ears and cranked up the music, flipping through my playlists until I found something appropriately intricate with decisive beats. With each rise of the music, I collected the magic, threading it into the song.

Then I cast it through the sprite and into the little stick figure. Seemingly enchanted by the pretties I'd added, and the magic, the spirit went without a fight. I focused my intent on the two things becoming one thing, binding the spirit to the poppet and the poppet to the spirit in an intricate spell that reminded me of a sort of spider's web.

My heart lurched. *Please.*

I gasped when the poppet moved on its own, little twig arms spinning in circles before it hopped out of my hands and bounced up my arm. The energy had given itself life—but I gave it a body.

"Totally creepy, but kinda cute." I told him as he hopped onto my opened palm. "Now, everyone can see you."

He ran up one arm then down the other, before flinging his new form into the air where my poppet danced and flew like a leaf caught in the wind. I'd felt his fear, his anger, and now...happiness.

"Poppet." Simple and fitting. "How does that sound?"

He shimmied a dance, wiggling his arms and legs before hopping up on my shoulder like he belonged there.

"Let's go 'fess up to Shelley."

Samhain, and Shelley's reaction, both went much better than I'd ever expected. We neared sunrise by the time I stood, gently swaying to the music, amidst Shelley's backyard fall wonderland.

A determined squeak turned my head around to where Poppet now bounced upon Eric's shoulder.

"I'm here to pick up the leftovers, and this guy seemed really insistent that I come out here." He picked the doll up with long, nimble fingers and inspected him. "Well done, Anna Bentley."

Pride in my magic wasn't something I was used to, and I smiled instantly despite being exhausted where I stood. "Thanks! He's calmed down a good bit already. I think...he just wanted to be seen."

Eric tickled his stomach with the tip of a finger. "He's cute in a sort of bizarre, creepy way."

"I said the same thing." I watched them. "Shelley says I created my own familiar. I think she may be right."

"Instead of a cat, you get a wayward poltergeist dancing around on sticks." He put Poppet on my shoulder sand grinned. "Neat trick."

I snorted. "Not hardly, but I like him." If the butterflies in my belly were any indication, Poppet wasn't the only thing I liked.

Poppet whistled this time, air pulling through the twigs.

"I think he's saying I should ask you to dance."

The warm tingling on my shoulder was most certainly agreement. I glanced at the adults to see that none of them were paying me any attention. Not being seen, it seemed, was the best idea for the moment.

"Well?" I cocked my head to the side and teased.

Eric slipped his hand in mine and pulled me to the flat stones serving as a backyard dance floor. A gentleman, he kept one hand on my back and the other gripped in mine. And before I could say anything, he winked, and a small gust of wind lifted us just off the ground and spun gently.

"You're not the only one with tricks, little witch."

Best day ever.

The End

ABOUT LESLIE

Award winning author of the Black Water Magic Series, Leslie Scott has been writing stories for as long as she can remember. The happier the ending, the better. Currently, she lives and writes amidst her own happily ever after with her soul mate, son, and domestic zoo.

www.lesliescottwrites.com

THE PERFECT BIRTHDAY GIFT

BETTY BOLTÉ

Northern Alabama – 1821

If she could have only one gift, she'd choose to be seen as well as heard instead of ignored and overlooked. Perhaps then she wouldn't be afraid and could force herself from her bed on this long-anticipated milestone day.

"Myrtle?" The question preceded rapping on Myrtle's bedroom door.

"Go away." Myrtle pulled the patchwork quilt over her head with a groan.

"Happy birthday, sister!" Merriment and anticipation threaded through Meg's tone. "Your special day has arrived."

"I'm asleep."

A snicker filtered through the wooden door. Cool fall air wafted from the partially open window into Myrtle's room, carrying the scent of the last roses from the garden. The Marple sisters' cottage nestled just off Winchester Road about a mile from where they worked as kitchen maids at the Fury Falls Inn. Inherited from their parents, they'd lived in the quiet domicile on their own for several years. But Myrtle missed her parents every single day. This day most of all.

"I have a surprise for you." The latch squeaked and Meg's footfalls scurried into the bedroom. "Come on, get up. Breakfast is ready and I need to give you this."

"I'm tired." The day before had been a busy one at the inn. Thankfully, they both had her special day off from work. A day her mother had once joked she'd find out about her destiny. Not likely. Just another drudgery day like all the others before and ahead. She clutched the quilt. "I need a few more minutes."

"Please." Meg's voice trailed off. "It may be important."

Meg's urgent whisper made Myrtle relent. With a resentful sigh, she flung the blanket off and climbed out of bed. Meg seemed over eager to greet her. Myrtle stretched her arms over her head, putting off the inevitable as long as possible, and then froze for a moment when she spotted an envelope in Meg's fingers. Letting her arms fall to her sides, she met her sister's gaze.

"What is that?" The pastel envelope came from her mother's personalized stationery.

Meg offered it to her with quivering fingers. "She made me promise to give this to you today. Once you'd turned twenty-one."

"You've had it all this time?" Myrtle stared at her sister's wary countenance. Meg the reliable, always the one tasked with the important things in life. "Keeping secrets."

"No, it's your birthday surprise." Meg shoved the missive closer. "Open it."

A letter from her deceased mother to be opened on her birthday. To say what? Maybe she was adopted, and her mother didn't want to tell her until she'd matured enough to handle such surprising news. Or maybe the letter contained something innocuous like simple birthday wishes. But why the delay of years to receive it? What was special about turning twenty-one?

Perhaps her destiny waited in the lines of the letter. She swallowed the nervous lump forming in her throat. Only one way she'd ever solve the mystery.

She inhaled deeply as she accepted the lavender paper, tearing the end off the envelope before she had time to think more about the act. Sliding out the single sheet, she opened it to skim the elegant script.

Myrtle, my little angel,

I am happy you've reached the age of 21! I wish you all the best of tidings on your big day. You should expect a very important visitor who will bring you something unexpected but hopefully welcome in honor of reaching this milestone in your life.

I wish you well and pray you'll use your gifts wisely.

Love always,

Mother

"What does it say?" Meg sidled around to peer at the writing. "Good news?"

"Maybe. Mother says to expect a visitor today." Myrtle glanced at the back of the letter but nothing more was written on the paper. "She doesn't say who or why, exactly."

"Bringing you a gift of some kind?"

"Mother does mention using gifts wisely, so I suppose." Staring longer at the words wouldn't help her understand their meaning any better. Better to go on about her day and try not to fret. She folded the paper and slid it back into the envelope. "I'll dress and meet you in the main room to break our fast."

During the time it took to don her day dress, fix her hair, and pull on her shoes, she could ponder the note's contents. Why her mother asked Meg to wait until her birthday to share the vague message. A shiver wiggled through her. A visitor. Something unexpected. Gifts. What did it all mean?

"I wonder when this person will arrive. I suppose I best prepare for having company." Meg spun on one foot and strode away, glancing over her shoulder as she paused at the open doorway. "At least your birthday won't be boring."

"Go on with you. I'll be along." Myrtle slowly shook her head as her sister turned the corner into the main room of the cottage. Most every day was boring. But perhaps boring would be better than an entire day filled with uncertainty and waiting. Perfect.

The day passed quietly, filled with expectation and interruptions. Myrtle repeatedly heard hooves or footsteps. Only, when she went to the front door, no one stood outside ready to knock. After the umpteenth time, she decided to busy her hands and ignore the outside sounds. At least she tried.

"It's late afternoon and still nothing." Myrtle stood from where she'd been working at the spinning wheel, winding a bobbin of thread from spun flax. She went to the window and pulled the drape open to peer outside. "Nothing."

"You're wearing a path in the carpet." Meg retrieved a platter from the sideboard in the dining area of the main room. "Relax. He'll get here when he gets here."

"I suppose." Myrtle let the drape fall back into place as she turned away from the window to let her gaze drift over the contents of their home.

Their house was in some ways typical of a laborer's cottage, and yet in other ways unique. Comprising four rooms—the main room with a kitchen and dining area to one side and a parlor grouping around the fireplace on the other, two bedrooms at the back of the house, and a scullery lean-to to store their dishes and utensils and other bits and pieces—she had been born in the bedroom she had occupied since her parents' death. She considered the abode something of an anomaly, having not only two bedrooms but two fireplaces for such a small home. Perhaps her parents had more money back when they built the place than in later years. She'd never know now that they'd passed on.

She and her sister hadn't changed anything about the furniture or furnishings in the cottage, preferring to remember the love their parents had bestowed upon them through the familiar chairs, tables, and dishes. Even the glass vases placed around the room, sprouting small bouquets of wildflowers from the surrounding woods, evoked fond memories of their mother arranging the dainty blossoms.

Myrtle crossed the room to stoke the embers into a cheerful snapping blaze in the parlor fireplace. The heat warmed her cheeks as she leaned over, poking and stirring the flames. Then she straightened to address her bustling sister, scurrying back and forth in the cozy kitchen. "So, what's for supper?"

"My roast hare and stuffing with baked apples and yeast rolls." Meg glanced over at her to gauge her reaction. "Sound good?"

"You're making me hungrier." She smiled at her sister's keen grin. "Need any help?"

"Not on your birthday."

"But…"

Meg shooed her toward a flower-patterned chair to one side of the fireplace. It had been her father's favorite, a family heirloom passed down from one generation to the next. "Enjoy my gift to you, a day off from home chores. Supper's almost ready."

"If you really don't need my help…" Myrtle stared into the fire, letting her thoughts drift. She tried to relax, the play of colorful flames enthralling her imagination.

What did her mother's note mean? What gifts should she use wisely? If only her mother were still alive, she could ask. How she longed to have her mother's counsel as the years flowed past, one like another. What did her future hold? A husband and children in a quaint house along a river sounded like heaven.

Though no man had shown her any interest in a very long time. Probably due to her usually chestnut hair changing seemingly overnight to gray. She looked far older than her true age. Now if the mysterious stranger could do something about that situation, she'd have a very special birthday gift indeed. She chuckled at the thought.

The flickering flames suddenly flared brighter and brighter, popping and snapping as they grew taller. Startled, Myrtle gripped the arms of the chair. "Meg!"

"Oh!" Meg fluttered closer, wiping her hands on an apron tied about her waist. "Get back."

The flames twined together, creating a vibrant braid of orange, red, blue, and white. Then it snaked into the room and burst into a rainbow of crystals that scattered onto the floor. In the middle of the strewn crystals stood a glowing woman with long black hair, replete in a shimmery golden gown.

"Who—who are you?" Myrtle jumped to her feet, grasping Meg's hand as she backed away from the ethereal being. Heart beating frantically, she stared at the strange woman. "Where did you come from?"

"Calm down, Myrtle. It's all right. I am Elswyth. I have waited a long time to make your acquaintance." The beautiful woman gently smiled as she glided toward her, extending an inviting hand. "I'm your elven envoy, my treasures. I'm here at your parents' request to inform you of your destiny."

Meg's grip on her hand nearly broke her fingers. Myrtle pulled her hand free but kept her gaze on the intruder. "I didn't know of an envoy of any kind, let alone... elven?"

"It's your birthday gift, my dear." Elswyth shrugged her fine shoulders as she continued to regard Myrtle. "Your parents told you that you'd learn of your destiny once you reached the age of twenty-one, didn't they?"

"To learn my true destiny." Her mother had been very specific about the correlation between her age and her destiny.

Not so specific about how she'd discover the truth. "Are you my destiny, then?"

Elswyth chuckled. "No. I'm here to instruct you on your gifts and reveal your heritage."

Myrtle gaped at the gorgeous if rather astonishing woman. Then she scanned the room, looking for any new items. None to be seen. "What gifts?"

"You won't find them in the room, my little treasure, but inside of you." Elswyth splayed her hands and then clasped them together. "You've been granted very great gifts, indeed." She raised a hand and gave a gentle flick of her fingers as she spoke words in a strange yet lyrical language. "There. Now you have possession of the gift of moving objects with a thought and the ability to sense magic."

"What did you do to her?" Meg stepped forward, angling her body in such a way as to become a shield from any danger the woman might pose. "Are you some kind of witch?"

"Oh, no. I'm an elf, just like Myrtle. And you, too, Meg, when you reach the age of twenty-one. That's when your powers can be freed for you to use." The woman arched a brow at them. "Not until you've become mature enough to handle them. That's for everyone's protection. I've been looking out for you and your safety all along."

"Wait. What do you mean I can move things with a thought?" Myrtle held up a hand as though trying to stop someone approaching too closely. Elswyth shot backward several paces before she regained her balance. Myrtle quickly dropped her hand to twine her fingers together in front of her trembling skirts. "I-I'm sorry."

A grin spread on the lovely elf's lips. "That's your strongest gift, your ability to move things with a thought. Excellent." She tilted her head slightly to one side as she regarded Myrtle. "Your gift is one of the most powerful abilities an elf can possess. You must use it wisely."

"Oh, my goodness. What if I hurt someone? I can't possibly… Will you teach me?" Myrtle held out no hope of learning on her own. She'd need to make big adjustments to grasp how to safely use her surprising birthday gifts. "Please?"

"Of course, that's why I'm here." Elswyth glanced at Meg and then back to Myrtle. "I'm also here to grant you one birthday wish. Anything you want." She held up an elegant hand as if prepared to conduct an orchestra.

"Anything?" So many options flitted through Myrtle's mind. A fine new gown. A pretty horse to ride. Maybe even a carriage and pair of horses. Then she and her sister wouldn't have to walk everywhere. But how would they afford such a luxury? She observed her sister out of the corner of her eyes for a moment. Her best friend and closest relative. The one who stood by her no matter what might happen. Then Myrtle met Elswyth's patient gaze. "I want Meg to have her abilities now instead of waiting two more years. She's more mature than I am even though she's younger."

Meg's wide eyes spoke volumes as to her feeling about the idea. Then she blinked in surprise. "Your hair. It's no longer gray but silver and…glowing."

Myrtle touched her head, long, soft hair beneath her fingers. The wiry mess she'd tolerated for several years was gone. "What happened?"

"Your hair has changed along with you to reflect your elvish nature. You now resemble your mother's true appearance and will inherit her birthright. You no longer need the disguising charm, so I've removed it. You're able to live your heritage now." Elswyth gazed at her for a long moment and then shifted to regard Meg. "Do you accept this gift from your sister? Realizing it will change your life in ways you can't predict."

The revelations came quickly. Disguising charm. So that's why her hair had changed so quickly. Myrtle fingered the silky tresses draped over one shoulder. Her hair glowed softly with an ethereal quality, hinting at the elven magic coursing through her veins. How would Meg change when she received her gift from Elswyth? Myrtle peered at her sister, searching for changes.

Meg drew in a deep breath and nodded once. "I accept her gift."

"Very well." Elswyth spoke several words in her lyrical language and then waved her fingers at Meg. "I grant you, Megara Marple of the Willow Forest people, use of your elven heritage and abilities."

Myrtle gaped at her sister as a soft white light appeared, brightened and sharpened into a flash of rainbow crystals, and then revealed her transformed sister. Her mouth fell open as she blinked in surprise. "You're beautiful, Meg."

"Am I?" Meg stared down at her soft hands, no longer worn and dry from spending days working in the kitchen. She met Myrtle's astonished gaze. "What do you see?"

"Your gray hair has become ash-blonde and floats about you like a cloud. Your skin is alight with youth and life like never before. But your eyes are the biggest difference."

"Why?" Meg touched her cheek as she stared at Myrtle with wide eyes.

"They look like rainbows." She'd never seen anyone with eyes of such a sparkling color. She turned to look at Elswyth. "Did my eyes change as well?"

"Yes, my dear. They also dance with energy like your sister's but with more green in them to reflect your genuine nature. Your name reveals much about who you are."

"In what way?" Her name represented a bush, after all. Short and squat, most likely, too. "Am I an evergreen?"

Elswyth snorted indelicately. "Not like a tree, no. But you will live a long and loving life. The myrtle has long been held sacred to Venus and thus is a symbol of love."

She shook her head, recalling how few boys or men had paid her any attention. "I rather doubt that."

Elswyth lifted her chin as ire flashed in her eyes. "Do not doubt me. I know what I am talking about."

"I apologize. It's just that…" How did one share how ignored she'd felt for so long? Invisible and forgotten. "Nobody notices me."

"Now that you've come into your gifts, your destiny, your heritage…that will no longer be the case." Elswyth smiled tenderly at her. "You will be noticed and respected by everyone from now on."

"What about Meg? I always thought her name was simply Meg but you called her…something else." She'd been shocked at how Elswyth had addressed her sister. "What was it?"

"Megara. It's an honor to be named after one of the Furies, my treasures." Elswyth smoothed the skirts of her filmy gown. "Not that I'd hope you'd behave as one, of course. The Megara of mythology punished those guilty of infidelity."

"Does it also reflect who I am?" Meg eagerly searched Elswyth's expression. "What can I do?"

"You now possess two complementary abilities to Myrtle's. Clear-knowing and the ability to control liquids." She peered at Meg for a long moment. "Not only will you receive intelligence, that is know things about those around you, but you can also control water like rivers and lakes and more. Like Myrtle's ability to move things with her mind, controlling liquids is a very powerful gift and can be dangerous. I will teach you how to use it properly and safely so it doesn't overcome you and leave you weak and defenseless."

"May I ask who the Willow Forest people are?" Myrtle searched Elswyth's tender expression. "Are they our ancestors?"

"They are your family, your roots anchoring you to this green earth." A gleam lit in her eyes as she regarded the sisters.

"They are the source of your gifts so never forget them, for they are keeping watch."

The sensation of being watched that she'd frequently experienced wasn't her imagination or any kind of paranoia after all. Rather, it was her family keeping her safe from afar. Now that she'd reached maturity, it was time to do more to protect herself and others.

"Thank you for our gifts, Elswyth." Meg grinned at their elven envoy and then at Myrtle. "And thank you for asking her to give me mine early. It will be far more fun for us to learn how to use them together.

"Yes, thank you, Elswyth." Myrtle glanced at Meg and then addressed Elswyth. "What more can you tell us?"

"What would you like to know?" Elswyth glided across the floor to perch on the edge of a matching flowered chair.

"Everything." Myrtle leaned toward the elf with anticipation simmering in her chest. "Tell me everything."

The next morning, Myrtle poured a cup of coffee and carried it out to the porch. Settling onto one of two carved wooden chairs flanking a round table, she surveyed the clearing in front of the house. The forest extended beyond and crawled up into the foothills of the Appalachian mountains, the trees slowly donning their spectacular autumn colors. A footpath snaked through the trees on its way to join the main road around a bend. The garden plot lay off to one side of the cottage, guarded by a lone willow tree draping its fronds toward the ground. All was quiet and peaceful. The view had not changed but she certainly saw things differently. The willow tree represented the connection to her people and thus far more than she'd ever realized before. She sipped the hot brew as noises from inside alerted her to Meg's rising.

The door opened and Meg stepped onto the porch, pausing a moment to inhale a deep breath and let it out. Leaving the door open, she padded across the plank floor to flop onto the other chair, and then placed a steaming mug on the table. "You're up early."

"I couldn't sleep." Myrtle slid a look at her sister and then returned to staring at the trees. "Yesterday was a bit much to grasp."

"Is something bothering you?" Meg propped her chin on a palm as she leaned on the arm of the chair.

She shrugged, gripping her cooling mug in both hands. "I have a feeling there's trouble brewing at the inn. Big trouble."

Meg sighed as she shifted to lean back in the chair, her gaze drifting across the clearing. "I heard something about women being murdered, women who lived alone."

"Yes, I did, too." Myrtle let a mouthful of coffee warm the chill threatening her core. "We live together and walk together to work so there's not as much of a threat to us."

"Especially now when we can take care of ourselves. Or will be able to once we learn how to effectively use our new abilities." Meg chuckled with glee before taking a long sip of coffee. "Still, we should be careful."

"After all that Elswyth shared yesterday, I still want to work at the inn. They need us." Thinking about the many revelations throughout the night kept her tossing and turning in her usually comfortable bed. "What do you think?"

The complete truth of who Megara and Myrtle Marple were still shocked her. Their parents had reigned the Willow Forest people for years before they chose to have a family. Then they'd stepped down, turning over control of their people to others while they'd left the forest to move to the little home and raise their children. Despite the king and queen walking away, the people continued to revere them for being kind and decent leaders. The Willow Forest people had agreed and decreed that the couple would always be king and queen and therefore their children would also be royalty. Meg and Myrtle were princesses of the Willow Forest realm.

Meg sipped, swishing the liquid in her mouth before swallowing. "I don't know how we'd help them, but it's better to keep an eye on things there. Something is indeed brewing."

"Is that your clear-knowing talking or something else?" Myrtle grinned at her beautiful sister before sobering. "Either way, we should go back and act like nothing has changed."

"Except our appearances. We can't deny that." Meg gestured to Myrtle's entire body. "You've had quite a transformation."

"How will we explain our new look?" Myrtle smirked at her sister. "We can't say our elfish envoy helped us."

"Elven, dear." Elswyth appeared on the porch beside Meg's chair, dressed not in her lavish gown but in dark green, leather leggings, an oversized, tan hunting shirt, and black knee boots. "Not elfish. That's rather insulting."

"My apologies. I was attempting a joke that has apparently failed." She gazed at Elswyth with a surge of love and joy swelling her heart. The elf's arrival changed all Myrtle knew about herself and her people. The knowledge led to her newfound energy and enthusiasm for life and those she cared for. "I appreciate you improving my appearance. Perhaps there is hope for me to find a man yet."

"Now, my little treasure, that has never been the case. The right man won't worry about how you look but how you act. Surface beauty is fleeting while inner beauty lasts a lifetime." Elswyth motioned to her attire with a slanted glance. "Is this too scandalous for this region?"

"I'm afraid so, even though it looks very practical and comfortable." Meg inspected the older elf's outfit with more interest. "Women wear ankle-length dresses and blouses in these parts."

"How old-fashioned of them. But it's better to fit in and not draw attention when in a new place. Very well." Elswyth waved a hand and with a few quiet words and a flash of rainbow crystals changed into a green skirt, tan blouse, and black leather shoes. "Better?"

"Are you going somewhere?" Myrtle hadn't thought to find out her plans. Where did an elven envoy sleep? "I thought you'd go home. Say, where is your home?"

"With you, my little treasures." Elswyth flicked her fingers again, a third chair appearing out of thin air, and then sat down. "With you."

"Really?" Meg leaned forward with a brilliant twinkling in her eyes. "You want to live with us? Here?"

"So many questions, my dear." Elswyth steepled her fingers, elbows propped on the armrests. "I think it vital to stay and make sure you're properly trained and know what is expected of you both."

Myrtle could only stare at her. The previous morning she'd awoken fearing the surprises her mother had hinted would occur on her twenty-first birthday. Never in her craziest dreams had she envisioned what actually transpired. Discovering she descended from an elven king and queen and thus she was a princess. But not just an elven princess. She had the ability to detect magic and to move objects with her mind. Her sister also had amazing gifts. And the relief that came with discovering they had enough money held for them so they could afford to live without worry. Only one question remained.

"Now that we have come into our heritage and destiny, our lives will obviously be different. However, we've decided to continue working at the inn so we can keep an eye on developments." Myrtle glanced between Meg and Elswyth. "But how do we go back to our routine knowing that not only will they see us differently but we'll act differently?"

Meg firmed her lips for a moment as she tapped a finger on the chair. "We just will. They'll have to accept us as we are."

"Tell them your aunt came to celebrate your birthday and brought you some special gifts." Elswyth winked at Myrtle. "That's close enough to the truth it should satisfy everyone."

"My hair?" Myrtle fingered the silken strands hanging over her shoulder. She'd not bothered pulling it up yet because she reveled in the new look and texture. "How do I explain that? I don't have any way to make it this color."

"If they didn't pay much attention before, maybe they'll just assume they hadn't noticed it?" Meg suggested. "We can hope that's their response."

"That's a good thought." Myrtle smoothed the glowing silver hair on her shoulder and smiled at her sister. "I'll make that observation if anyone bothers to ask."

"So, we have a plan." Meg sat up straighter and smoothed her long lynsey-woolsey skirts over her lap. "We'll continue to help the cook at the Fury Falls Inn and keep our eyes and ears open as to why women are being murdered in this area."

"And be prepared to help anyway we can." Myrtle squared her shoulders and pinned Elswyth with a smile. "While you stay here to run things and teach us more about how to control our gifts."

"I could use a break in my usual activities. But I'll be right beside you should you need me to help at the inn. Just call my name and I'll appear." Elswyth folded her hands in her lap as her grin faded. "I can tell you're both worried about the future. As well you should be. I, too, sense something brewing."

Meg pushed to her feet. "If something really is coming, then it's time we learn how to control our abilities and prepare to confront it. Ready?"

Elswyth arched her brows. "Now?"

"Why not?" Myrtle stood as well, tapping one foot until the

envoy also pushed to her feet. "There's really no time like now. The sooner we know how to use our gifts, the better."

Elswyth shrugged once as she moved a few feet from the table. "We'll start with something easy." She pointed to the half-empty cup on the table. "All you need to do is think about what specific object you want to move where. Move that cup."

"Don't I need a wand or something?" Myrtle stared at the cup, perplexed by the vague instructions. How exactly was she supposed to move an object with her mind?

"You're not a witch. You don't even need your hands, just the thought. Of course, you can embellish the importance of the act by using gestures, but that's all about being a showman." Elswyth gestured to the cup with a flick of her hand. "Keep it simple. Try."

Myrtle concentrated on the cup, intent on lifting it. Staring at the small vessel, she thought about where she wanted it to be. After several seconds, it wobbled and then shot upward into the air, crashing into the porch roof and shattering. Meg covered her head with her arms and backed away as the pieces and cold coffee showered onto the table and floor boards. Elswyth disappeared without a sound and then reappeared standing on the grass in front of the porch, arms crossed and a frown on her face.

"Up-a-daisy." Myrtle grimaced as she glanced warily at her instructor's unhappy expression. She'd really bungled her first attempt, much like a child falling when learning to walk. "What did I do wrong?"

"You need control. Don't just picture the cup in the air, but think of it rising slowly and with a purpose. Now try again."

"You can do it, Myrtle." Meg eased closer to lend her sisterly support. "Go on."

Myrtle focused on Meg's cup and followed Elswyth's suggestion. The cup rose up and up and then hovered about two feet above the table until Myrtle set it gently back down. She shot a grin at Elswyth. "How was that?"

"Much better. Let's try something larger." Elswyth skimmed her gaze around the porch. "One of the chairs?"

Convenient if a rather boring idea. She met her sister's quizzical gaze and had another idea. "Meg, do you want to go for a ride?" Myrtle smirked at her sister, daring her with a pointed look.

"Um…" Meg took two steps back from the nearest chair. "I don't know."

"I will be careful, I promise."

"What do you think, Elswyth?" Meg wrapped her arms around her waist.

"We must help her learn quickly, so if you're fine with doing it, then I approve." Elswyth darted a warning glance out the corner of her eyes at Myrtle.

"I'll be careful. Come on, Meg, sit down." Myrtle held the chair for her sister, urging her closer with a smile.

Meg reluctantly sat down and held onto the seat with both hands. Myrtle moved around in front of her sister and aimed a reassuring grin her way. Then she thought about lifting the chair and its occupant a few inches from the floor until the chair did as she wanted. Meg smiled at her but tightened her grip on the wooden seat while Elswyth clapped her hands in approval. Myrtle made the chair angle this way and that like it was performing for the audience, then slowly spin around in place before setting it down.

"You've learned very quickly." Elswyth grabbed Myrtle in a hug, holding her tight for several moments. "Your parents would be so very proud."

A wave of pleasure and pride swept through Myrtle at her praise. "Thank you. I never imagined I'd have such a wonderful gift. I feel as if I could do anything I put my mind to."

"Just be careful you don't inadvertently move something at

an inappropriate or even precarious time. You must both marshal your thoughts to prevent accidents or, worse, disasters."

"Does that mean it's my turn?" Meg stood up from the chair and walked to the edge of the porch. "I need water, but we don't even have a puddle."

"Any fluid will do. Even the remains of your coffee." Elswyth climbed back up the steps to peer into the other cup. "There's enough to work with."

"Does it work the same for me as for Myrtle?"

"Yes. Just think what liquid you want to go where. Focus on doing so with control." Elswyth stepped back from the table as Meg moved into position to stare at the cup.

Myrtle shuffled off to one side so she could see without interfering. Giving Meg space both physically and emotionally to try her hand at applying her new gift. She held her breath as her sister moved into position.

Meg gazed at the cup until slowly the dark liquid snaked upward, writhing and twisting in the air before splashing back into the vessel. "I did it!" Meg spun around to face Myrtle with a gleeful expression. "I followed your example and it worked. What a feeling, knowing I can do that."

A sliver of jealousy poked at Myrtle's ego, but she snapped it in half. Her sister may have bested her feeble attempts, but Meg had always been a tad faster, sharper, better. Despite being younger, or more likely because she was used to observing how Myrtle did things and finding ways to improve on the technique or approach. "I'm so proud of you. Nicely done."

Meg hurtled herself into Myrtle's arms with a squeal of delight. "Isn't it wonderful?"

Myrtle gave Meg a last squeeze before easing from her excited embrace. "What exactly?"

"Feeling confident and powerful instead of meek and ignored. Just like you said." Meg grinned at her, bobbing her head several times as she folded her arms. "I feel transformed, like a butterfly emerging finally from its chrysalis."

"You're right, Megara." Myrtle crossed her arms over her chest and smiled at Elswyth and Meg. Her birthday gift had ultimately transformed her both outside and in. "We no longer need to fear others but can use our gifts to help them. What a perfect birthday gift to us both."

The End

ABOUT BETTY

Betty Bolté is known for authentic and accurately researched American historical fiction with heart and supernatural romance novels. She has published more than 25 books of fiction and nonfiction topics, most recently Becoming Lady Washington: A Novel, Notes of Love and War, and Fractured Crystals (Fury Falls Inn Book 4). She earned a Master's Degree in English in 2008, emphasizing the study of literature and storytelling, and has judged numerous writing contests for both fiction and nonfiction. Get to know her at www.bettybolte.com. Be sure to check out materials for book club discussions at https://www.bettybolte.com/bookclub.

FRIDAY AT MAPLE HILL

BONNIE GARDNER

Vonnie Wright was late. If she didn't hurry, she wouldn't be able to talk to Nathan this week. Since he'd been there, she'd never missed a week.

She reached for her purse and car keys just as her cell phone rang. Groaning at the delay, she accepted the call as she hurried out the door. "I can't talk. I'm on my way to Maple Hill."

It was her daughter April. "But Mom, my babysitter cancelled, and I have to be at work by five. I'm already late. You only have to watch Sweetie until Doug comes home."

April had just started a temporary job that was to last through the Christmas season, but the money she earned would take their savings account to the total they needed for a down-payment on their first home. Vonnie had offered to help, but Doug had insisted they do it themselves.

She sighed. "All right, but I'm going to take Sweetie with me. There's a playground there, so she can play on the swings. It's warm today. I'm on my way.

"Oh, and what time do you expect Doug to be home?"

"He's usually there by 6:00. I left a casserole in the fridge. You can put it in the microwave when you get back."

Vonnie ended the call. As much as she loved helping with Sweetie, her four-year-old granddaughter, she needed to keep reminding April that she had a life. Well, not so much since Nathan passed, but she still had friends and plans and things she wanted to do.

At least, April's apartment was on the way.

Though she had always enjoyed the fall colors and the Halloween decorations, Vonnie sometimes hated the month of October because the plants she loved began to disappear one by one, victims of the changing season. Still, she enjoyed the last blast of color until darkness returned soon after Halloween.

Vonnie had always enjoyed watching children in their costumes as they paraded through the neighborhood, stopping to ring the bell and demand, "Trick or treat." It bothered her that fewer kids came every year.

What happened to the joyous celebration of autumn and harvest before the deep darkness of winter fell? She had looked forward to it every year when she was a child, pondering mightily on what to wear and how to make her costume special. Why had people come to see it as sinister and dangerous?

Yes, night fell earlier this time of year, but it was nature, not evil, she thought as she started the car.

The headlights came on automatically in response to a thick overcast that seemed to have come up out of nowhere. Technically, the sun hadn't yet set, but it would soon be dark.

April and Sweetie were waiting in front of the apartment, and she wasted no time tucking Sweetie into the booster seat in the back. "Thanks, Mom. You're a lifesaver," she said as she slammed the door shut and turned toward her own car.

Of course, Vonnie didn't have time to wait around either. Fortunately, the traffic moved quickly as she drove counter to the flow of homeward-bound workers, and they reached Maple Hill in time, though she had only a few minutes to visit.

Instead of using the parking lot, she parked close to the

paved walkway that led to the Wright's family plot in the old section of the cemetery. Shivering in the sudden chill, she reached for Sweetie's hand as they walked to Nathan's spot, but Sweetie dashed toward the small playground on the cemetery grounds.

"I wanna go to swing," she announced as she sped away.

Vonnie didn't really understand why the playground was there, but it was, and she wasn't going to question it.

"I see some kids," Sweetie called.

Vonnie started to go after her but decided to let her go play. The playground was in plain view, and she'd only be with Nathan a few minutes. She walked quickly to her destination, carrying the bouquet of colorful flowers she'd picked from her own garden.

"Sorry I'm late, honey," she said as she stooped to clean up the remains of last week's offering and replaced it with a fresh one. She would drop the dried stems in a waste can near the road when she headed home.

"April's sitter fell through, and she had to hurry to work. Remember, the kids are saving for the down-payment on their house," Vonnie told him.

"It won't be long till the garden is done, Nathan, but these are still pretty," she murmured as she placed the new bunch in the cement receptacle. "The mums are going strong, so I might bring you a potted one next time."

There was a bench near the plot, close enough to see Nathan's spot and contemplate, and Vonnie sat for a moment, enjoying the quiet. The gleeful shouts of children at play interrupted the solemn silence, and Vonnie glanced toward the playground. Seeing another woman there apparently supervising her own children, she assumed Sweetie would be all right for a few more minutes.

The autumn clouds sagged lower, and a chilly mist drifted over her, seeming to sink into her bones and make the air feel colder than the balmy 59 degrees the thermometer at home had suggested. Odd how much warmer it was under the normally bright rays of the sun. Vonnie flexed her knees, wincing at the audible creak that seemed to echo in the lowering darkness.

Regretting her aching bones, Vonnie pushed herself up. "I guess I have to go, Nathan. It's starting to drizzle. Maybe next time, I'll be able to tear Sweetie away from the playground and give you a chance to see how much she's grown. She's in Pre-Kindergarten in school this year and pretty soon she won't be our little baby anymore." She blew him a kiss and headed toward the playground.

As she neared, the happy laughter of children playing made her smile as she watched the swings fly to and fro. The other woman, of a grandmotherly age, wearing what appeared to be a summer dress, stood watching, one hand on her hip.

"They look like they're having fun," Vonnie commented, pulling her sweater closer around her.

The other woman turned and smiled. "Yes, they do."

"That's my Sweetie, the one with the curly red hair. Are the other ones yours?"

She shook her head sadly. "No, mine are too old for that now. I just enjoy watching the children play when I come out to see my husband."

"Yes, they do look like they're having lots of fun." Vonnie glanced toward a fence on the other side of the playground. "I wonder where their parents are. It's pretty late for them to be here alone."

"Oh, they're around," the woman answered breezily. She seemed unaware of the chill.

"Well, I'd best get my granddaughter back to the car. I don't want her to catch a cold. She had a bug last week and missed a couple days of school." Vonnie glanced at the other woman. "I expect you're getting pretty chilly, too."

"I hadn't noticed," the woman said. "Sometimes I forget how quickly it cools down this time of year."

"I don't," Vonnie confessed. "My creaky knees remind me every day." She turned to where Sweetie was swinging as high as she could. "Come on, Sweetie Pie," she called. "We need to go so we can get supper cooking before your Daddy comes home."

"Oookay," Sweetie answered reluctantly, dragging her sneakers through the packed sand to slow down her momentum. The swing came to a grudging halt, and Sweetie slid off the seat and stood up.

"Let's go," Vonnie called impatiently. "Gramma's creaky knees want to get warm."

"You could wear knee socks," Sweetie suggested sagely as she caught up with Vonnie.

She chuckled. "Maybe I will next time."

"Can I come with you another time?" Sweetie asked hopefully, her angelic face turned up toward her. "I like playing with those kids."

"Maybe we can." However, Vonnie hoped that April would solve her babysitter problems before then.

"And you will wear socks and push me on the swing?"

Vonnie laughed as one last shaft of sunlight slipped out through the clouds. "We'll see."

Sweetie turned and waved, but when Vonnie looked to see who was waving, the playground was empty.

It was the week before Halloween and Vonnie found herself bringing Sweetie to Maple Hill again. The sitter had a bad cold and wasn't sure if she was contagious.

This time they arrived earlier, and the sun had not quite sunk below the horizon, though it was barely visible above the tree line.

Although it was warm with the last rays of sun still peeking between the trees, Vonnie had thought to dress in a pair of wool slacks. She always wanted to look her best, and she dressed up when she visited her husband even if she had gained nearly a dozen pounds since he'd passed. She parked the car so she and Sweetie would walk past Nathan's spot before Sweetie ran off to the swings. "Would you like to carry the flowers?" she asked before Sweetie could dash away.

"Okay," the girl replied, grabbing the small pot of florist mums. The frost last weekend had finished off most that were growing in Vonnie's garden, so store-bought would have to do till spring. Sweetie trudged ahead and plopped the pot carelessly down and turned toward the swings.

"Don't you think you should, at least, say hello?" Vonnie reminded her.

"Hi, Grandpa. I'm sorry you're dead."

"That's not very nice. Don't you think his feelings might be hurt?"

"No, he doesn't mind. He smiled at me and said I could go."

"Smiled? How do you know?"

"I see him. Wite dare." Sweetie pointed and backed away. "I wanna go to swing now." Then she spun around and hurried off.

"I guess she doesn't remember you well, Nathan. She was only two when you passed, but you have to admit she has quite an imagination." Vonnie smiled as she adjusted the placing of the flowers, gathered up what was left of last week's offering, then settled on the bench. "She is growing like a weed, though."

Not expecting Nathan to answer, Vonnie was content to sit and remember, or maybe imagine a conversation. Soon the joyful sounds of children playing interrupted her thoughts, and she smiled. "I guess I'll have to go now. I promised our grand-daughter that I would push her on the swings."

Although it wasn't as damp as the last time she'd come with Sweetie, Vonnie noticed the chill as she wandered toward the playground. The same woman was there again, in the same light, summer dress. Was it her only nice dress?

"I'm afraid I won't be able to bring Sweetie to play on the swings much longer. Maple Hill will start closing at 4:30."

The woman turned abruptly as though she'd just heard Vonnie approach. She forced a weak smile. "I suppose not."

"My name is Vonnie Wright, by the way." She figured she'd introduce herself if she was going to keep running into the woman. She stuck out her hand.

"Denise," the other woman replied, her hands tucked under her arms in the chilly afternoon. "Your granddaughter does seem to enjoy playing here," she said, sounding far away.

"I suppose so. Her family lives in an apartment. It's not very child-friendly, and she doesn't have a playground.

"My daughter and son-in-law are saving for their first home, and Sweetie is hoping for a swing set of her own."

"That will be nice," the woman agreed. "I do miss having young ones around." She turned back toward the children playing on the swings.

Her phone rang, and Vonnie excused herself and answered. "Oh, hi, Doug. Sure, that's great." She put the phone away and turned back to Denise.

"My son-in-law will bring home pizza, so I don't have to cook anyth—" she started to explain as one last ray of sunshine peeked out from behind the trees, but the woman had disappeared.

"Oh well. Some people are not good at ending a conversation," she murmured out loud. She glanced at her watch and shrugged. It was time to go anyway. She turned toward the swing set and noticed that the other children had gone, as well, leaving Sweetie by herself.

"Let's go, kiddo. It's getting late," she called.

"But Grandma. You promised to push me."

Vonnie smiled. "Yes, I did. We'll stay just a few more minutes and then we have to go. Your daddy said he's bringing home pizza," she circled the swing set and positioned herself behind Sweetie.

"I like the kind with cheese in the crust. Push me high as the sky, Grandma," Sweetie called.

"Sure, Sweetie Pie," Vonnie replied, having no intention of doing so. She gave a few perfunctory shoves, enough to get her granddaughter's curly hair flowing in the breeze, and then called a halt. "We better go. That pizza will get cold."

"Okay," Sweetie agreed reluctantly as she dragged her feet until the swing slowed, then she quickly stood. "Let's go."

Sweetie hurried toward the car, stopping at Nathan's spot. "Bye, Grandpa. My Daddy is bringing pizza for supper." Then as the last ray of sunshine dipped behind the tree line, she scurried after her grandmother.

Vonnie glanced once more in Nathan's direction and noticed Denise at another grave a short distance away. She supposed that the woman had someone to visit as well. She waved and Denise waved back.

Then she urged Sweetie toward the car.

That April kept needing a babysitter at the last minute was beginning to annoy her. Vonnie loved her granddaughter, but it was Halloween, and she had planned to go to the cemetery early so she could get home and prepare for the onslaught of ghosts and goblins coming to the door.

Vonnie and April waited at the corner of the parking lot, ready to leave as soon as the school bus dropped Sweetie off. April would rush off to her job and she and Sweetie would go to see Nathan.

She'd fashioned a little Halloween-themed arrangement to place on Nathan's spot. Though he hadn't been as fond of the season as she was, he'd tolerated her fixation with the fall holiday.

Finally, the big yellow bus pulled to a halt, and Vonnie and April waylaid Sweetie as she jumped off. "Come on, we're going to see your grandpa again," Vonnie said, squeezing her in a hug.

Sweetie, still wearing her costume from her class Halloween party, shrugged out of Vonnie's embrace and grinned. "Good. I can show Grandpa my costume and see the other kids, too. I wonder what they'll be wearing."

"We'd better go, or it will be too dark soon." It was bad enough that clouds hung low and dark again today. Why it was always cloudy on Friday afternoons, she didn't know. It almost seemed as though the sky was playing its part for the big night.

April took Sweetie's book bag and confiscated a sack full of goodies and turned toward the apartment, presumably to put them away.

As Vonnie headed toward Maple Hill, she asked, "Did the other kids at school like your costume?"

Sweetie shrugged. "I guess. I wanted to be uh orange-striped cat, but Momma made me be a black one instead."

"I like orange cats," Vonnie stated. "They have red hair just like you." She reached over and ruffled Sweetie's thick, red hair.

Tucking a piece of candy that she had apparently sneaked out of her bag into her mouth, Sweetie made a face with one bulging cheek.

"Well, I'm sure Grandpa will like your costume."

Soon they arrived at the cemetery, and Vonnie parked the car and helped Sweetie out. "We won't be able to stay long this afternoon," she said, glancing up at the glowering sky. "We have to hurry home to get ready for Trick-or-treat.

"Odd," she murmured to herself as the trudged along the walkway. "I don't remember the weatherman saying anything about rain."

Running ahead, Sweetie stopped short when she reached

Nathan's resting place. She pirouetted, holding her hands out to keep her balance. "Hi, Grandpa. See, I got a cat costume." Then she turned abruptly and headed toward the playground.

The same group of kids were playing there, and Sweetie joined them, hopping on the one vacant swing. Again, Vonnie looked around for anyone who could be supervising them. It was early enough in the afternoon that they could be outside, and there were houses nearby, but it bothered her that they always seemed to be here without any responsible persons keeping watch. Especially, since she didn't see Denise today, either.

Vonnie placed the new pot of mums in the cement holder and settled on her bench to talk to Nathan. As she sat, she caught a movement in the corner of her eye and looked up to see that Denise was visiting a grave not far from Nathan's.

She waved, and Denise gestured for her to come over.

Quickly saying goodbye to Nathan, Vonnie pushed up off the chilly bench and wended her way over to where the woman waited. She stopped short when she realized that a man was there, kneeling at a gravesite, his white hair highlighted by a thin shaft of sunlight that had broken through the clouds.

"Oh, hi. I'm sorry to disturb you." Vonnie turned and realized that Denise had slipped away.

The man, probably just a few years her senior, glanced up. "I've seen you here before, so you're not exactly a stranger.

"Is there someone special you come to see?"

"Yes, my husband Nathan. He's been here a couple of years now." Vonnie pointed in the direction of the Wright family plot.

"I've noticed the fresh flowers every week." The man smiled, and something inside Vonnie felt warm despite the impending darkness.

"I come to visit my wife, DeeDee. It was four years last summer." He smiled sadly. "My kids say I should move on, but how do you do that when you spent all your adult life with one special person?"

Letting her sweater coat fall open to tame a sudden flush of warmth, Vonnie smiled back. "I understand. My daughter says I should get on with my life, as well. That coming is a bad habit, but to me it's been hard to break. It's comfortable and familiar."

"Kids! What do they know?" The man smiled again and pushed himself to his feet. "Name's Pete Petersen," he said, offering his hand.

"Hi." Vonnie felt another odd surge of heat run through her as she grasped his hand. "I'm Vonnie Wright. Nice to meet you."

"Same here," Pete said. "Say, it's getting a little chilly here. How about joining me for a cup of coffee over at the café across the road."

"That would be so lovely," Vonnie replied. "But maybe some other time. I have to get my granddaughter home to get ready to go trick-or-treating."

"Oh. I thought you were alone."

Turning toward the playground, Vonnie explained. "She's over there on the swings."

"Oh, I see her now. In the cat suit."

"That's the one."

"Well, how about we plan to get coffee next time we're here?" Pete suggested.

"Well, thank you," Vonnie replied, blushing. "I'd like that. Next time, then," she said.

"It's a date." He turned and headed to where a car was parked not far from hers.

Vonnie waved at Sweetie, and she trotted over, apparently, ready to go since the prospect of trick-or-treating beckoned harder than the kids on the swings.

"Did the other kids like your costume?"

Sweetie shrugged. "I don't know. They didn't say. They

didn't have costumes on. They always seem to have the same clothes on every day."

"Maybe they go to a school that has uniforms."

"I don't think so," Sweetie replied. "They don't all match like umi-forns. They're more fancier than school clothes, anyway."

Vonnie glanced toward the playground, but the kids were gone. Now that she thought about it, it had been a long time since she'd seen girls in skirts and ankle socks and boys that wore button-down shirts and vests. "I guess the kids went home. I suppose they're in a hurry to go trick-or-treating."

"Yeah. I'm in a hurry, too."

———————

The first Friday in November dawned clear and crisp.

The sun shone bright in a robin's egg blue sky on a warm, Indian Summer afternoon. Funny, Vonnie couldn't help thinking, how the weather had changed for the better once Halloween had passed. It was almost as if sun that had been in hiding was ready to portend something new.

She didn't have Sweetie with her this time. April's babysitter had promised to be on time, and Vonnie had taken her at her word. Besides, she had a sort of date with Pete Peterson, and she didn't want to be late.

Should she call it a date? It had been so long since she'd been a member of the dating world, that she wasn't sure. Since she'd been married and widowed, the rules for dating had changed, at least for young people. She wasn't sure if the ones she'd followed when she was going out with Nathan more than forty years ago still applied.

It was just coffee, she reminded herself, but when was the last time she'd sat and enjoyed the company of a man? Had she read too much into the casual invitation?

Still, it felt like a date to Vonnie.

Amazing how welcoming the cemetery appeared today, she thought as the blue sky and white clouds made it look more like a park than a cemetery. For the past month or so, it had seemed that, even if it had been clear in the rest of the city, clouds and gloom had hung over Maple Hill like a shroud. Or had it just been her imagination as she contemplated the coming Halloween festivities?

Whatever the reasons, Vonnie appreciated the change.

There were more cars in the small parking lot today. Probably because of the nicer weather, Vonnie supposed, but she still found a vacant slot and pulled in. Eager to leave her weekly floral offering for Nathan and then ... meet with Pete?

Would he be there, or was she making too much of an offhand suggestion? She glanced ahead and didn't see him. And, she realized, she didn't see the children this afternoon either, though the playground seemed to have been recently abandoned. The swings still rocked to and fro, and the merry-go-round was just coasting to a halt.

She didn't see Denise, either.

Still, visiting Nathan was her primary mission for the day. She carried a small bouquet containing colored leaves and just a couple of bright orange and yellow mums. She smiled as she looked down at them. Frost had nearly ended her flower garden, but she'd been fortunate enough to gather a few hardy chrysanthemums that had managed to hide from the cold.

She smiled. Some years the weather would remain mild and dry into December, but she expected that would not happen this year. It had already been cold once with what had not quite been a killing frost. Still, that first blast of cold, strong enough for coats, usually meant that what passed for winter in north Alabama would soon blow in.

The Halloween-themed bouquet she'd left the previous week looked dry and faded, and Vonnie picked it up, replacing it with the new one she'd prepared. She knew Nathan had never really cared about flowers, but she felt as though she couldn't come with nothing. He'd given her so much throughout the years.

She settled on the concrete bench, warmed by the bright November sun, and thought about all the years they'd been together. Of course, Nathan had liked the fall for football season, but not because of the colors. Unless you considered the orange and blue of Auburn football. She chuckled. He'd probably prefer a gift of Iron Bowl tickets, not that he'd be able to use them. Or maybe now he finally had the best seats possible.

She smiled.

"What's so funny?"

Vonnie looked up and saw that Pete had appeared at her side. "Oh nothing. I was just thinking that Nathan would probably have preferred Auburn colors rather than all these fall flowers I've been putting out."

Pete sank to the bench beside her. "Oops. I guessed I should have asked if I could join you."

"Please," Vonnie said. "I don't own this bench, and you're welcome to sit."

"So, your husband was an Auburn fan?"

"Since he was in junior high." Vonnie smiled. "I never really understood it," she confessed.

"Don't tell me you are an Alabama fan?" Pete remarked, looking shocked.

Shaking her head, Vonnie confessed, "I never understood the rabid devotion to football teams, at all. It's just a game."

Pete clutched at his heart, feigning shock. "You didn't grow up in Alabama, did you?"

"Army brat. I grew up all over the world. Never had the opportunity to build an allegiance, I guess." She shrugged. "Nathan tried to convert me, but I hated wasting fall afternoons I could be spending gardening by watching other people play a game."

"You don't normally tell people that, do you?"

Vonnie felt herself blush. "I learned not to soon after moving here when I was in high school." She sighed. "I try to remain as neutral as I can, even if I did go to Auburn because it had a good horticulture program, and I wanted to work with flowers," she felt it necessary to confess.

"That explains all the pretty flowers you're always bringing."

Blushing at the realization that he'd noticed, Vonnie went on. "Just a hobby now. I owned a little flower shop and green-house for a long time, but I didn't have time for the greenhouse after Nathan got sick. When I realized I couldn't take care of him and run the store, too. I sold it." She smiled wistfully. "Sometimes I wish I hadn't. There are still times when I need something to fill my days."

"Heard that," Pete agreed. "I retired just before DeeDee passed. We'd planned to see the world."

"Oh, was it sudden?"

"Yes, she had an aneurism. How do you prepare for that?"

"For a long time, I didn't see the attraction in world travel," Vonnie confessed. "I did it most of my childhood, but now I…" She stopped short.

"Wait a minute. I thought your wife's name was Denise. Isn't that what was on the stone you were visiting?"

"Yes, I was the only one who called her DeeDee. It used to annoy her." He grinned. "So, I kept calling her that. When we bought the plot, she made me promise not to put it on her gravestone." He smiled sadly.

For a moment, Vonnie thought about the coincidence that had brought Pete to her, but then she smiled. Appreciating the good luck, she was certain that it had been DeeDee who had brought them together.

She looked over at Pete who gazed pensively in the direction of DeeDee's stone. After a moment he seemed to jerk himself back to now, and he smiled. "You know, my family says that I've spent too much time at this old cemetery. They want me to get out and maybe meet somebody."

Vonnie smiled. "I understand. My daughter has been saying the same thing."

Pete pushed himself to his feet and offered his arm. "Well, it's not too late to get that cup of coffee I suggested last week. Are you ready?"

For the first time in many years, Vonnie placed her hand on the arm of another man and smiled. "Yes, I think I am."

Funny, as the sun sank behind the trees, Vonnie thought she heard someone call after them.

"Have a good time."

The End

ABOUT BONNIE

Bonnie Gardner is a former army brat and air force wife. She is a Master Gardener and loves growing her own mostly-organic vegetables. She lives in northern Alabama where she can visit with her grandchildren as much as possible. She is the author of more than 30 books.

Most are available at Amazon and many e-book venues.

Email: author@hiwaay.net

KIDNAPPED FOR A DAY

CARLA SWAFFORD

A Circle Organization Short Story

"Shut up." A voice bellowed from the shadows of the Sandbox Bar and Grill's parking lot followed by the sound of flesh hitting flesh.

Then a distinct feminine whimper penetrated the predawn morning silence.

Luke Warren's orders were to wait until Emma Cooper got off work at two and then *try to save* her from the staged attack by one of his men. Physical violence had no part of that plan. Since he'd seen the other three waitresses leave minutes earlier, that left only her.

He growled in frustration beneath his breath. They had been instructed to go easy on her. The idiot was to frighten her, not mistreat her. Taking a second to control his temper, he marched around the corner, preparing to play his part. His boss knew how he felt about mistreating women.

For Christ's sake, he had two sisters he loved and never

wanted involved in his life. Thankfully, they had enough sense to remain safely at home with their spouses. His life was so different from the way they lived theirs. However, recently his job had brushed up against his youngest sister's best friend's life. That was, her brother's clandestine life.

Another slap pierced the air.

Damn it. That had to end. He was going to tear apart the asshole limb from limb.

As his eyes adjusted to the darkness, a huge shadow moved beneath a busted security light. Luke stopped and watched as the mass separated and took shape. The man loomed over a much smaller, curvy silhouette as he squeezed her upper arm. The woman covered her head with a free arm in a protective stance.

The man wasn't one of his.

With practiced ease, Luke palmed his Glock 43 from the holster in his boot. As he double-fisted it, he edged around a truck and halted.

Scrutinizing the man, Luke noted he didn't have a weapon. So he slipped his gun back into his boot. No need to escalate the situation with the threat of gunfire. A good, old-fashioned fist fight was what he needed. As the bastard raised his hand to strike Emma again, Luke darted forward and slammed into the man's torso. With a grunt he landed on top and the man's head hit the asphalt with a hollow *thunk* and then the asshole remained motionless.

Luke recognized the thug. He belonged to Mikolas Savalas, a crime lord out of Atlanta. Where the hell was his guy?

A sick feeling swirled in his stomach. His employer had warned him Savalas and his people could be sniffing around. They were a tricky bunch, who would do anything to get one over on The Circle, the private military organization Luke worked for.

He pressed two fingers to the side of the unconscious man's

throat. Relieved to feel a steady pulse, Luke slipped out a roll of Velcro zip ties from one pocket and nylon zip ties from the other. Then he flipped the unconscious man onto his stomach. Most people would think it strange he always carried a supply, but in his line of business being prepared could mean the difference between life or death. Anyway, they didn't take up a lot of room. He made quick work of entwining the ties around the man's wrists and ankles, effectively hogtying him. By the time the unconscious man woke and worked them off, Luke should be long gone.

Luke rose to his feet and turned toward the woman.

Cupping the side of her face, she grimaced and stared wide-eyed at the thug. "Is he dead?"

A few seconds ticked by before he realized he was staring. He blamed it on the beer he'd downed before leaving the bar and the early hour of the morning. He'd forgotten about her beautiful eyes.

"Emma." Time to put on his tarnished white knight armor and play the gruff hero. "What the hell are you doing in this side of Sand City?" All part of the act.

Luke's gaze traveled with consternation over the petite brunette with her one cheek slightly swollen, but not as bad as he expected. He lightly brushed his knuckles across the forming bruise.

"I work here." Her voice wobbled.

"Don't you know better than to walk out alone at this time of night?" Guilt sent a chill through him. The bartender had been paid to stay behind.

Emma opened her mouth to reply, but when her gaze lifted, her eyes widened, focusing on a point past his shoulder. She gasped. He pulled his gun, and began to swing around, but a flash of light sent him to his knees followed by massive pain as blackness closed around him.

Luke lifted a hand to rub at the pulsating ache at the back of his skull. He jumped when a jingling waterfall of chain slapped his face. Squinting, he gingerly turned his head to glare at the restraint. Oh, hell. A thick manacle encircled his wrist. Welded to possibly three feet of chain, it was attached to the cot's rail, and likely the legs were bolted to the cement floor.

Thick, humid air filled his lungs as he gasped for breath, panic mounting with each second.

No, not again, he silently screamed. Using all of his concentration to regain control from past traumatic memories, he inhaled and exhaled. Inhaled. Exhaled. Over and over. He slowed each exhale to quell the initial panic. He knew the cell well. Each crack he'd counted many times. The metal door's window was too small to crawl through even if the rusty bars were brittle enough to crumble away. Buzzing fluorescent tubes from the hallway provided the only light. He'd spent eleven hellish months wasting away in the square cement block space.

Whose joke was it placing him there? He would break their neck. If not for the knowledge that The Circle organization had taken control of the former Savalas compound after his escape, he would be freaking out. The obvious reason his confidence held was that he still wore clothes. Savalas loved stripping his captives.

As he regained his composure, blinking away the grit and hated past, he checked out the rest of the cell. The only change was the figure huddled in the corner. *Damn it.* What had they done to her while he'd been out? Sure, they needed to make it look realistic, but why knock him out? And what was up with the chains? And bringing him back to this place?

"Emma," he croaked. He cleared his throat, then tried again. "Emma."

She lifted her head, revealing dark half-moon smudges

beneath her eyes from smeared makeup and lack of sleep. Bruises and tear-streaked cheeks finished the pitiful picture, but she raised her chin, pulling herself together.

Good. The woman had guts, but he hated seeing the bruises.

That wasn't to happen.

Then he spotted the metal collar. Cursing beneath his breath, he sat up, clutching his own chain. The assholes went too far. He was well aware his organization would execute any abuse to get the information needed. But did they not understand how delicate the woman was?

"Who else hit you? Did they touch..." He stopped his line of questioning when she dropped her face into her hands and shook her head, sobs racking her body. He was an idiot. She didn't need his interrogation.

Curling his fingers, he hoped he could resist punching the next person to show his face.

The few times he'd been around Emma, she'd been quiet, modest, polite, and sweet. No one with her innocence should be pulled into the middle of the craziness he dealt with more often than he wanted to think about. Sure, time was limited, and experience had taught his organization that by placing someone in an unusual, harrowing situation, the person would promise a first born in exchange to return to their everyday safe life. Still, she hadn't deserved to be treated so cruelly.

Glancing her way again, he squeezed his hands into fists. Desire to caress her cheek and ease her worries tightened his chest, but she needed to stay anxious. Otherwise, he would be defeating the purpose of the mission. But he guaranteed they'd never touch her again. Clanging brought him back to his situation. *Damn chain.* He yanked at it and waited, giving her time to manage her feelings as he passed the time imagining ways to tear apart the person who moved from intimidating to terrorizing an innocent.

After a few moments, her weeping slowed. Then she wiped away her tears with a torn sleeve.

"I-I don't know. I mean they shoved me into a big SUV, bruising my arms, hip." She rubbed her right side. "But they didn't try, you know." She blushed, and dipped her head as she pulled at the collar with a trembling hand. After a couple of minutes, she gave up the effort to rid herself of the collar and eased to her feet, swaying, causing the chain connected to her collar to jingle.

"Be careful or you'll faint. I can't help you from here." He shook his manacle as he scooted across the cot until his back rested against the wall. "Come, sit here, if your chain reaches this far. Go slow. Don't want you to fall." His voice maintained an even tone in an effort to lull her to trust him. "Take it slower."

She slid one foot and then another while grasping the chain. When she reached the cot, she became tangled and landed half on, half off the thin mattress.

He reached for her, but came up short. *Stupid ass chain.* How many more bruises could the woman endure? "Are you all right?"

Rubbing at her left hip, she pulled herself up until she also sat leaning against the wall, a few inches separating them.

"I'm a little clumsy but okay. Nothing like matching bruises." Her eyes welled up and spilled over though she remained quiet. She blinked away the tears. "Sorry. I can't seem to stop crying."

Unable to resist any longer, he moved as far as his manacled left hand allowed and placed his free arm around her shoulders, squeezing her to his side.

"I know this looks..." —he glanced around as a chill raced down his spine— "bad, but I swear we'll get out of this and soon." The tremors from her body almost matched the pulsating pain in his head and neck.

Hell, she didn't deserve to be in the current screwed-up mess.

Without even thinking about it, he kissed the top of her head. Surprise washed over his torso. He wasn't the sort of guy to cuddle, not even with his sisters, but she brought out his protective side times two.

It didn't make sense. She wasn't his type.

He preferred tall, slender blondes. Emma was the total opposite, but strangely, her height-challenged frame suited his perfectly. Having her soft, rounded body tucked into his felt so right.

She sighed and leaned harder into his side, her head resting on his chest.

"What do they want with us?" She sounded like a lost, little girl, her eyes wide to the point they looked as if they might pop out.

"It's not you. It's me. I escaped and they wanted me back." His eyes closed for a few seconds in frustration. All the lies driven by the necessary setup felt so wrong, but his story had to make her feel responsible for his current predicament. It was part of the job. He needed her scared, just not to the point of being petrified. "You got caught in the middle."

"Why take me? Why me?"

He stared down into her sweet face. What was one more lie?

"They'll release you when they come back to question me."

Her gaze searched his face. She wouldn't be able to read anything he didn't want her to. He'd been told many times he was a good liar. That he could make a fortune playing poker. Yet, he never gambled. Why should he? He gambled with his life on every mission.

Unable to resist it any longer, he leaned down and swiped a thumb over one tear-stained cheek and then the other. The silkiness of her skin triggered his cock to harden, lengthen. Hell, the last thing he needed was having her feeling awkward, but he could stop his response to her nearness as much as he could stop his hands from moving. As in, not at all. He appreciated the silkiness of her skin beneath his fingertips as they traveled down her neck and across her collarbone. His strokes wandered along her arms, over her soft curves until he stopped at her thighs, hovering over where her legs joined.

Though her tremors stopped, her face changed to a pretty pink. Her eyelids drifted half closed. She enjoyed his touch as much as he savored touching her. No fear shimmered from the depths of her warm eyes. Her lips parted with a sigh.

Damn, those kissable lips.

Admittedly, he'd noticed her full lower lip before. Perfectly suckable. But moving around, working dangerous assignments, and keeping his business private from his only family necessitated he ignore his desire for the sprite in his arms. So difficult to stay away. Especially as she was his sister's best friend. What was the chance of him finding another one like her? She'd never want anything to do with him after she survived their ordeal. Just his luck.

He groaned and bounced his head against the wall. They'd loosened something in his brain when they hit him. That had to be why he acted so maudlin.

———

Emma melted against Luke. Really, how many women could resist snuggling up to a broad-shouldered, long-legged man with such inscrutable gray eyes? She certainly couldn't. She barely managed to stay away from him even with his sisters' warnings of Luke being a heartbreaker.

Besides, he always looked at her with politeness. Well, until he woke up in a cell with her.

She rested her head beneath his chin and closed her eyes, soaking in the comfort he offered. As his hands roamed over her, she struggled to keep her breathing even despite the rapid beat of her heart. When he hesitated at her upper thighs, she swallowed a gasp. Her surroundings disappeared as every nerve in her body centered between her legs.

The clank of metal hitting metal down the hallway and a whiff of fresh air warned that someone was coming. She snapped out of the lust-induced trance his touch had created.

Luke's massive body stiffened beneath her.

In response, she started to tremble again, but he quickly wrapped a muscular arm around her waist and squeezed tight in a mixture of warning and protection, dragging her onto his lap. A calmness came over her. From the tidbits told by his sister about his interest in martial arts, he was capable of handling any frightening situation.

His chain rattled.

How could he fight with one hand hampered?

Unhurried heavy footsteps approached from down the hallway.

Part of her wanted to move away from Luke before their captor came to the cell. Yet, deep inside, she wanted to remain in his embrace. Safely tucked against his warm body. She reasoned even an independent, confident woman like herself loved a strong man willing to protect her.

Then again, how embarrassing being caught embracing while on a man's lap. And really, they had to look a total wreck, what with her bruised face and degrading collar, and Luke with blood dried from his temple to ear, matted in his hair and spattered down his light-blue T-shirt. Dirt coated a strip of his shirt and on down one side of his jeans. Probably left over from when he attacked the asshole who had hit her. She didn't want to think of how she smelled. The cell's human waste stench was bad enough and probably had already seeped into her pores.

Maybe she should move. She closed her eyes, incapable of

making a decision at that point as she continued to soak in his comforting touch. What did it really matter?

The weak light in the cell dimmed even more as someone partially blocked the small, barred opening in the door.

"Welcome back, asshole," the deep voice said.

She made out only a silhouette of a perfectly shaped bald head. Not many men were lucky enough to have one. Then white teeth appeared, like the Cheshire Cat, almost glowing in the low light. Shudders ran down her body.

Goodness, she was going off her rocker. Who cared about the shape of his head or how shiny his teeth? She warily eyed the man.

"Where's Savalas? I expected his greasy ass." Luke lightly squeezed her waist as he used a threatening tone.

Was he telling her he would do his best to protect her and she needed to be quiet and play along? Not that she was a mind reader, but he had tried to save her from the attacker. His sisters swore he had a white knight syndrome.

Thank goodness.

Syndrome or not, she allowed herself to relax against his hard, virile body. She'd never experienced having someone willingly place themselves between her and danger. Yeah, she had loving parents and a solicitous brother, but she didn't remember anyone actually protecting her. No one had ever acted worried about her well-being.

"He's busy. He sent me to take out the trash." He leaned back from the opening. Then she heard a beeping sound as if he'd punched a code into a keypad.

The door swung open, allowing more light to pour through as the man stepped inside. His head nearly brushed the top of the metal door frame. Baby-blue eyes appeared to glow, not with a fanatical shine, but more with total amusement at the situation. He hung back enough to keep more than the chain length away.

"Considering I was gone and then you brought me back, that's all on you, asshole," Luke said, each word coated with scorn.

Why was Luke provoking the man?

In the dim light, she narrowed her eyes to more closely examine the thug. He had piercings in one eyebrow, both earlobes, and bottom lip, and when he crossed his arms, his T-shirt stretched across defined pecs and biceps. Tattoos peeked out from around the neck and below the short sleeves, covering his forearms and hands. He was a good-looking man, but something about his tone revealed a hardness of spirit from years of disappointment.

She pressed against Luke's chest.

"Actually, we needed *you*." The man's gaze dropped to her face.

"Me?" She squeaked. Luke was wrong.

Her head swam. She'd always wished to be brave, but when push came to shove, her backbone would cave. That moment was no different.

Why was she a coward? Her parents were kind to her growing up and her brother rarely teased her. Her family always called her a dreamer and she agreed. She loved to read anything with romance and fantasy in it. She was the ideal, helpless damsel in distress and she didn't care what other people thought. Luke certainly needed women like her so he could be a successful knight in shining armor. From everything else she'd heard from his sisters, Luke was courageous and a bit of a daredevil.

Maybe that was part of why he attracted her.

"Yes. Dickhead here got in the way. We need you to tell us where your brother is. He has something we want back."

She knew it! She loved her brother, but he constantly stirred up trouble despite promising not to involve the family in any of his shenanigans.

"Emma, tell them what they want to know. They'll let you go," Luke whispered in her ear. The scuff on his jaw lightly scraped her cheek causing her to shiver.

How did he do it? Was it the mysterious danger surrounding him? None of the men she dated since meeting Luke had compared. He was such a man's man.

Pulling her head back, she looked into his eyes. Concern reflected in his ruggedly handsome features as his gaze met hers. He'd proven he would protect her, but at what cost?

Returning her attention to their captor, she nodded. "I'll tell you if you release Luke first."

The man smirked.

"What the hell?" Luke shook his head. "No. That's not going to happen, Emma. They don't bargain." He cupped her cheek with a big hand as his gaze met hers. "I appreciate the gesture, but don't worry about me. Do as he says. That's the quickest way to return home."

"No. If they want information from me, they need to agree." Where was her nerve coming from? She appreciated his concern. Scared silly, she somehow kept her voice steady despite how much her body shook.

The man shifted in the doorway and cleared his throat. "He's right. No negotiation. I'll give you two hours to hash it out. When I return, you'd better be cooperative." The clank of the door closing brought a mix of relief and dread.

"Look at me, girl." Luke's voice colored each word with sadness and desperation. "These people aren't messing around. You have to cooperate and quickly. The next time he asks, tell him or they will make you, and you don't want to go there. I'll take care of myself. Remember, I escaped their clutches before."

"Then I'll escape with you." What was coming out of her mouth? Obviously, being in his arms made her daring. Maybe she had a little of her brother's spirit in her.

"Emma—" He stopped talking, stared into her eyes for a

moment. Then he covered her mouth with his. Tongues tangled and stroked. Heat coated her from head to toes.

Wow. She'd never been kissed so thoroughly.

He squeezed her tight like she was about to slip out of his hold. Such a wonderful sensation. He kissed as if she could provide their last breath. Her hands caressed his chest and shoulders as if they had a will of their own. Threading her fingers into his hair, she sucked on his lower lip. His groan vibrated through her. Short of breath, she let go and leaned back.

"Sorry. Did I hurt you?"

He chuckled. "No, baby. But you're so much more than I ever imagined."

"Yeah?"

"Oh, yeah." He leaned his forehead against hers. "But this isn't the time or place."

"I—" She nipped at his swollen lower lip. Never had she ever acted so daring, but the fullness tempted her to take another taste. "I guess I could lie about where my brother is."

"No. Don't lie. They'll check before releasing you. If they don't spot him, they won't be as nice the second time they ask."

With a tilt of her head, she narrowed her eyes. "You're a lot like my brother."

"I'm not sure I like being compared to your brother after that kiss."

She giggled and covered her mouth. Where did that come from? She wasn't the type to giggle. Laugh, yes; giggle, no. After a sigh, she said, "He's not very forthcoming with his life. I know he travels all around the world, but never brings back pictures or fun stories like everyone else. Your sister and I have talked about how much you two have in common. Except I think you lied to your family about your destinations, unlike my brother. He knows I don't have anyone if something happens to him. So he makes sure to leave a note with his contact info."

A strange expression crossed his face.

"What's wrong?" She placed a hand on his shoulder. Did he feel bad about how he treated his sisters' anxiety?

Using one finger, he slid it across her brow, brushing strands of hair out of the way. An innocent touch, but such a turn on.

"Nothing. I think your brother is lucky to have a sweet sister like you, and I think you've proven you can tolerate bad situations."

She smiled. "True. Despite what he thinks."

"Let's get comfortable and talk some more." He shifted to lean his back against the wall. Her arms automatically circled his waist and her cheek landed over his heart. A tugging on her hair surprised her. He carefully untangled her hair with his fingers. "I'm not about to let you get hurt again." His voice rumbled beneath her ear.

"I guess you'll need to get us out of here."

His chest rose and fell with a frustrated sigh. "No. It took me eleven months last time. They'd have that exit covered. Besides, I need you safe before I try anything."

She pushed away and slipped off his lap to sit next to him. A feeling like a fist squeezing her heart sent panic racing through her. How could she choose? "So I have to pick between you or my brother?"

He lifted up her hand. "No. Between *you* and your brother. I don't count in this scenario." The press of his lips against her palm caused a wonderful tingling to shoot up her arm. "Please, baby. You don't understand how much danger you're in. Think about it. We have a little time. Here."

He placed her hand on his chest and she leaned against his shoulder. Solid and safe. That was Luke Warren. His sisters loved him dearly. She understood why. He would be easy to fall in love with, but like her brother, trusting and loving someone else besides family would be difficult for him.

She knew he was right, but her brother was the only person alive who loved her. How could she betray him?

Luke covered her hand with his, waiting for her decision.

Scum of the earth. Yep, that was him.

Probably an hour had passed as they leaned against each other and listened to each other breathe. Time was running out. She had no business being there.

"Your sisters are going to worry about you if they let me go and not you." Her eyes glistened in the dim lighting. Her voice was husky with emotion.

Please don't cry. I'm not worth it. "They'll be okay. They believe I have an out-of-country assignment. It usually keeps me out of touch for six months."

"What is it you do?"

"If I told you, I'd have to kill you." Not quite true, but she reacted like so many other people did, assuming he was teasing.

She sat up and slapped his arm. "That's horrible. Quit kidding. Your sister said you're involved with consulting work, but she never said what type."

"I consult on military weapons training."

"That sounds almost sinister."

With a shrug, he used the momentum to put his arm around her and pull her in tighter, returning her head to rest on his chest again. She felt good there. It was like his soul had found his better half. Her sweetness helped to comfort him. The brightness shining out of her eyes shoved all of the horrible things he'd seen and done back into the dark recesses of his mind.

"Strangely, normal." The lie came out too easily. He rubbed his cheek across the top of her head. "The meetings are often set at really nice resorts. I've never been the type to take pictures of

KIDNAPPED FOR A DAY

the places. That's why my sisters don't believe me. Does your brother send pictures?"

"Nah. But since I knew he was working, I never thought to ask. Besides, I never look at the notes he sends me, but he always returns around the date he told me before he left." She yawned. Considering what her body had been through and the inactivity for the last hour, the strain was catching up with her. "I wish I had a book to read."

"So you're saying I'm boring?"

"No. Just the last book my brother sent me started off really good," she mumbled.

He tensed at her comment. "He sends you books often?"

"Huh? No. Uh, it's kind of rare for him to do that." Her voice drifted off on the last word.

She was lying. That had to be the way he contacted her. Maybe if he got her mind on something else.

"I love to read, too. Usually westerns. What type of books do you like to read?"

"Anything with romance and fantasy." She softened against his body.

They talked for several more minutes before their jailer showed up with enough noise to wake the dead, the door swung open with a final clank, and the big guy walked in.

"Hello, lovebirds. Anyone want to live another day?"

She gasped and began to shake again. *Damn it.*

Why couldn't Jack Drago show up a little later? He wanted to confirm what he'd guessed. He glared at his accomplice. They had worked a few missions together and normally got along, but the big guy persisted in rubbing him the wrong way in their current assignment.

Luke hauled her onto his lap and wrapped an arm across her chest to her opposite shoulder.

"Check the book on the nightstand at her house on Swan Street," Luke said, as he tightened his hold and covered her mouth with his other hand. "It should be a romantic fantasy. A sealed note should be in it with his address." About halfway through his betrayal and her squealing, she bit his hand. He hissed with pain, but finished providing the information. It had to be done. The Circle was known for mercilessness. No way would he allow anyone to hurt her.

Jack nodded. "Shouldn't take us long to pick it up. We'll likely know where the asshole is before nightfall. If the info is right, she'll be released then."

Emma began to wail louder, still muffled by his hand. Then she wiggled, trying to break free without much luck as she was stymied by his constraining embrace.

Luke lifted his chin in understanding. He waited until Jack left before freeing her.

She continued her attack but with more vigor, striking his arms and stomach as she proceeded to talk about his parentage. Ignoring her to check on his hand—the hits were no more than playful thumps—he was relieved to see no blood. The little vixen. Then she slapped his face. Hard. The woman had a healthy swing. He clasped her wrist as another slap came at him again.

"Enough, Emma." Almost nose-to-nose, he enunciated each word carefully. "I understand you're mad, but I told you I wouldn't let anyone hurt you. Giving them the information will prevent that. I feel certain your brother can take care of himself." He dropped her arm and tensed, expecting her to hit him once again.

She scrambled to her feet. The chinking of the chain hanging from her collar irritated the hell out of him. Why hadn't he insisted on the asshole removing it? They should've never placed it around that delicate neck in the first place. The prick had done it to intimidate her. An overkill in his opinion.

Scooting to the edge of the cot, he tested the position of the chain attached to his hand. As he guessed, unless he wanted to stand with one shoulder down, he might as well stay seated. Feet on the floor and the back of his knees against the edge of the cot, he spread his legs and patted the mattress between them.

"Come here, baby. Nothing will be solved by you standing there. It's hours before dusk." The sadness on her face almost had him telling her everything would be okay. But how could he promise her that? Who could really predict the future?

"I should've never trusted you." She grimaced.

He held out his free hand, palm up. "Please. Let me hold you."

"You're a real bastard, you know that?"

"Yeah. You're not the first to say that. But I need you in my arms. I'm afraid." Afraid she would never let him hold her again. If The Circle killed her brother, she'd never forgive him. He couldn't lose her.

She blinked and opened her mouth to respond but nothing came out.

His statement had obviously surprised her. Hell, it surprised him. Many times he'd thought as much, but it was the first time he'd spoken it out loud.

Tears streamed down her face as she shuffled to the cot and crawled into his lap. They held each other with all their might for a good minute.

"You don't play fair. I'm still mad at you." She sniffed, swiping her sleeve across her cheeks, and relaxed.

A deep, long sigh escaped his lips. Damn, she belonged there. He loosened his hold and leaned back against the wall, arranging her cheek to press against his sternum. She belonged in his arms, just like that.

"Sorry, baby. Your safety is important to me. Your brother has proven he can take care of himself. He wouldn't approve of you endangering yourself further."

He kissed the top of her head and squeezed her as if his life depended on it. In a way, he felt like it did. He never believed a woman could take over his every thought in such a short time.

Why had she affected him at that point? Why not when he'd seen her at his youngest sister's house? Was it the tears? Yes and no. He'd always hated it when his sisters cried, but it was different. She'd demonstrated she had guts, the necessary willpower to stand up to those who threatened her.

Damn. What was he thinking to fall in love with her?

———

Emma woke with a start. The steady thumping beneath her ear along with the rise and fall of his chest felt so good. She closed her eyes again and immersed her senses into the moment. Just knowing the firm chest belonged to Luke Warren soothed her. Even his betrayal of her confidence couldn't destroy her feelings for the mystery man. In spite of the previous harrowing hours and how she'd come to realize he was flawed, she still wanted him.

Lifting her head, she stared into the face of the man who meant so much to her. From the dark aura surrounding him, she suspected his work was as dangerous as he was, but she was careful not to let her imagination run wild. Except at night, in bed alone. Then he'd been the lead in all of her fantasies.

The clang of metal down the hallway alerted her to their time coming to an end.

"Luke, wake up. He's back."

"I'm awake." He clasped her head and touched his forehead to hers as he whispered, "Whatever happens next be ready to run. Don't look back, don't worry about me. It's late afternoon. So run toward the sun. There's a busy strip of interstate about three miles from here. You can do it. Flag someone down and go to the nearest town. I'll make sure no one follows, but you still need to keep going forward. Remember that. Do you understand me?"

The desperation in his voice emphasized how important it was she follow his instructions. He had escaped before. He knew what to do.

"What about you, my knight?" She traced his lips. She didn't want to leave him alone. What if they killed him?

"Knight, huh?" He grabbed her hand and kissed it. "Listen to me. I'll be fine. I'm too valuable for them to kill. You need—"

"I have good news for the sweet thing." Their jailer opened the door with his usual clang.

"Take the collar off her," Luke demanded.

"All in good time." The man smirked as he took in their closeness. "But I have a couple more questions for the little fire-cracker. We need a little alone time." He bent down and unlocked the chain from the ring in the floor, leaving it attached to her collar.

Her skin crawled from the man's lingering leer. Obviously, he wasn't referring to alone time with Luke.

The man came nearer, slowly drawing closer by wrapping the chain around one fist. Before she knew what was happening, Luke shoved her to the side and bear-hugged the jailer, bringing them both down in a tumble of limbs onto the cot.

"Go!" Luke shouted as he head-butted the man and then hit him in the face twice.

Her collar jerked as the chain became entangled with the bodies. Then she was free. That was, she had the whole length of chain. Remembering what Luke had said, she gathered up the links and looped them around her arm. Without wasting another second, she skirted around the wrestling men and through the open doorway. Panic filled her when she heard shouting, but she somehow found the exit. No one was around. The oddness of no guards would have to be figured out later.

First, she needed to escape. Then she would find a way to help Luke.

By the time she spotted the interstate, she was exhausted. Slumping behind a huge bush, she unwound the chain from her arm and wrapped it around her waist. Somehow she needed to look normal. Otherwise, no one would pick her up.

Luke stood in the shadows of the open doorway and watched Emma run through the field of knee-high grass toward the interstate.

"Damn, man, why did you hit me?" Jack leaned against the door frame and fingered his jaw, a large, purple bruise quickly forming.

"It was bad enough you brought me to this hell hole and chained me, but you did the same to Emma."

"Hey, you know how the boss is. He felt the stress would heighten the realism." The bald man flashed his signature bright, devilish smile. "It worked, didn't it?"

Ignoring the question, Luke tilted his head, his gaze staying on the woman sprinting toward freedom. "Maybe I should follow her and make sure she's picked up like we planned." Rubbing his chest, he squinted as she became a dot in the distance.

"Don't worry. She'll be fine. Rick'll make sure she gets home."

"Rick. That pervert? I thought you said Katerina was doing it."

"She was sick this morning."

With Emma out of sight, he let his gaze move to Jack.

"Morning sickness?" Luke lifted his eyebrows. When they had met up to plan the mission, the big guy had mentioned they were trying for a kid.

KIDNAPPED FOR A DAY

"Yeah. Keep it to yourself. I don't need my father-in-law breathing down my neck about his first grandchild. Damn, it's going to be hell enough when he finds out." Jack tilted his head, a popping sound echoing down the empty hallway. Then he cracked his neck in the opposite direction.

His father-in-law was the very same dangerous crime lord, Mikolas Savalas, who had captured and imprisoned Luke. Every time he thought about Jack having to deal with the man every holiday, he cringed.

Luke's gaze remained on the horizon where Emma had disappeared. "When she finds out I set her up, she's going to be pissed. Maybe I should explain." He hoped she continued to be a forgiving woman.

"You might have to get on your hands and knees and beg, if you do." Jack chuckled.

Luke nodded. "She's worth it."

Without another word, he started walking across the field. About midway, he broke into a jog. He needed to hurry. The woman was too trusting and who knew what trouble she could find herself in again.

Yeah. The last twenty-four hours had been life-altering for sure. Who would've ever guessed a bum like him would fall in love?

No denying it. She was totally worth it.

The End

ABOUT CARLA

Carla Swafford loves romance novels, action/adventure movies, and men, and her books reflect that. And on top of all that, she's crazy about hockey, and thankfully, no one has made her turn in her Southern Belle card.

So, it's no surprise she writes spicy romantic suspense filled with mercenaries, motorcycle one-percenters, and southern criminals. And in the last few years, she's included sexy hockey players in books without suspense, except for the kind that asks, how will they ever find their happily ever after?

Married to her high school sweetheart, she lives in Alabama. To find out more about Carla, go to her website at carlaswafford.com.

REMY'S REUNION

CS WARD

A squad of woodpeckers hammered his head to mush. Remington Boudreaux nursed the hangover from hell. His innards gurgled; the south Alabama sunlight stabbed his eyes. He wasn't sure if he wanted to puke or just go on and die.

Thank God it was Saturday. Still, a workday. He sprawled on the shady porch gingerly sipping black coffee, even though it was closer to high noon than sunrise. No matter the time, there was still a full day's work to do.

When he'd clomped down the stairs, his mother had taken one look at him, and silently handed him the huge mug she'd just filled. "You might as well sit out there and drink this. It's a beautiful day. You can let me know when you're able to eat," she'd said.

Ma knew the signs, but it had been a long time since she'd seen them. He thought he'd left that part of life back in his high school days. Normally Remy didn't drink, but his two best friends were leaving for Marine boot camp next week. Jimmy and Jack were brothers of his heart as they grew up together. Remy was an only child but the three of them had been inseparable.

The evening before, they'd gone to have beer and pizza. But they'd had a few too many. They'd all realized this might be their last evening together and tried to celebrate all the future evenings in one. They closed down the place, and a friend had taken them home.

These days, you didn't let your best friends leave for the possibility of war or a vacation to Fiji without the proper send-off. You might never see them again.

They had started out with good intentions. All had work to do on their family land, even his departing friends. Fortunately for Jimmy and Jack, they had younger siblings to keep their farm going while they served the country. With the double J's, as they called themselves, Remy had not missed having siblings.

Then Remy's dad had died. Since then, Remy had to buckle down and work on the farm every day after school and full time on weekends. He'd not been able to hang out with his friends as much when the farm became his responsibility. Only by working his heinie off had he graduated from high school and the local community college majoring in Ag so he could run his farm. He had to keep his small farm going single-handedly. When he'd needed help, he'd swapped out with his friends. Everyone needed a hand sometimes. But that had been work time, and not hang-out time. It worried him that his two best buds were heading off to Parris Island. He prayed they'd return safely. He could manage his farm, but he couldn't manage the rest of his life without his two friends. It was going to be lonely without them to talk to and debate sports.

Long ago he had military ambitions, too. The three friends planned to go off and save the world. They were a little vague on what they were going to save it from, but with the cockiness of youth, they were determined. At the age of sixteen, they'd all been immortal, but Remy didn't feel immortal anymore. His father had been his biggest hero but had died way too young. He'd had a heart attack out on the tractor one day. Remy had been working with him, but despite getting him to the hospital within fifteen minutes, there had been nothing left to work with. Pop had worked himself to death. He hid his symptoms and wore a smile every day.

Pop had known he was not going to make it. "Take care of your Ma and the farm," he'd said. "I'll love both of you forever." Then he closed his eyes, and that was it. Even heroes had a shelf life.

Remy took his father's words to heart and threw his entire soul into the farm. He made sure Ma had everything she needed. He had to rethink his plans for college, sports, and professional football.

He frowned and tipped the last of the coffee into the rose-bush. It was as bitter as his thoughts. He didn't mind being a farmer. He just didn't want to spend life alone. "Pop, I'm sorry I failed you," he muttered.

The tractor sputtered. Remy tried to goose it through the coughing, but the motor shuddered to a stop.

Damnation, was the day intended to be a total waste? He was sweaty, dust-caked, and those damned woodpeckers were still pounding away behind his eyes. It had been years since he'd had more than one beer on a Friday night. Now he remembered why.

He climbed down and examined the tractor. Right there. Busted fuel line. No fuel left. He was a farmer, not a mechanic. At least this was something he could fix.

Now he had to hoof it back to get his battered farm pickup, fetch the new fuel line and fuel, then come back and work on getting the tractor to run. It was going to be a bitch to start up again. He didn't think he'd get much done during the remainder of the day after doing the repair.

There was nothing for him to do but start walking across the uneven dirt, and head for the barn.

———————

Sophie jerked when the car strayed off the road onto the ragged shoulder. She wearily steered it back, glad that the uneven road kept her awake. Only seven miles to go. Law school had taken forever and demanded sacrifices. After she got home this time, no more traveling. She'd settle down to be a small-town attorney.

She worried about fitting back in with the country community where she was born and raised. Some said you couldn't go home again. She hoped that wasn't true. Thoughts of home had sustained her through law school. Emory had been tough. However, she was confident she was up to the practice of law. She'd enjoyed the city because she'd known it was a temporary condition. Going home had always been her plan. She'd had no trouble passing the bar exam, which translated into several wonderful offers for her in Atlanta with salaries to match. But inside, she was still a country girl. She'd adapted to the city to finish her education. Now she was thankful to go home.

And yet, would any of her former friends be left to reestablish relationships? She didn't want to be alone. If all her friends were married with children, they wouldn't have much in common. If only she'd had time to think about her future a little more before returning to start earning a living. With demanding classes and study time, she hadn't been able to keep in touch with any of her friends. She feared they'd all gone separate ways. She hadn't really dated, although she'd admired one or two guys from afar. She remembered her secret high school crush then resolutely put him out of her mind. He had to be married by now with a flock of children.

She scrubbed at her grainy, wet face again. The car air

conditioner had given up the ghost long ago. So much dust came in the windows that her face was raw from wiping sandpaper sweat. Even the fan vents were bombarding her with dust. She aimed the airflow down. Better to be hot than blind.

Suddenly, she spotted the creek where kids had come to cool off for generations and realized she was close to home. It was cool and shady, and too tempting. Perhaps it could be a brief respite and allow her time to think. She was so miserably hot she felt like a piece of meat coated in batter, starting to sizzle in the deep fryer. On impulse, Sophie eased the clunker off to the side of the road. When her passenger wheel dipped into a dried rut, she heard a scrape. That couldn't be good. But it was too late to rethink her decision. Committed now, she climbed out of the car and glanced under it. *Like I even know what to look for,* she thought wryly.

Despite a niggle of doubt, she was going for a quick dip before driving the final short distance home. She'd come back and deal with the car and the rest of the trip home, if only she could rest and cool off for a short time.

She popped the trunk and looked for something to wear for a dip in the creek. It occurred to her she hadn't owned a swimsuit in years. The one she'd had was so faded and out of fashion she'd tossed it out. She hadn't had time for much recreation at school. She rummaged in her bag then withdrew her hand. Getting clothing wet and repacking it didn't appeal.

What the heck? It wasn't skinny dipping if you wore *something*, right? Unlike other high school friends, she'd never been part of that rite of passage. Besides, there was no one around, and a quick dip would be fine in her underwear. It was thin and would dry quickly, even under clothing. The air was stifling and silent except for the monotonous buzz of insects. With the brush crackly-dry, she'd hear anyone approaching.

She yanked her beat-up folding chair out of the trunk and hauled it down the scraggly path. It had seen her through many cram sessions when she wanted badly to be outdoors but the best she could do was studying outside. She was glad she hadn't left it behind. Tall grasses on either side swayed in the slight breeze. It didn't look like anyone had come to the creek recently. The dusty path was overgrown and void of human footprints.

Before she could talk herself out of it, she slid out of her clothes and tossed them over the chair.

In no time, she was stepping into the clear water. Oh, heaven! What a relief it was to slip her tired feet into the cool water. She wiggled her toes to discourage tiny minnows from tickling her feet. She stood motionless and closed her eyes. Glorious relief flowed through her as the stress washed away.

The creek wasn't as deep as she remembered; perhaps there had been no rain for a while. She waded down the middle of the stream to a deeper spot and submerged herself. She rose only enough to take a breath before sinking into the blessed relief again. For a few stolen moments, she didn't worry about anything or anyone.

Sophie thought she heard a motor near her vehicle, but she no longer heard it. Either it had stopped or was gone. It was time to head back anyway. She started for the bank and realized she was farther from her clothes than she'd thought. Then the sound of someone clomping down the path made her pause.

"Well, isn't *this* a fine howdy-do," she muttered as she moved faster.

Bounding quickly up the bank, she put on her shirt, leaving the tails dangling untucked around her thighs. She fastened her button-fly, cut-off shorts, then turned in the direction of the approaching footsteps to meet a man's carefully neutral gaze.

Oh, no! Her face flushed when she recognized her secret

high school crush. How in the hell did Remy Boudreaux show up here when she was vulnerable and disheveled? Had her thoughts conjured him? Sophie schooled her expression to mirror his. After all, *he* didn't have any idea she'd had a crush on him. She just had to brazen it out.

Remy had gone less than five miles toward town when he spotted the unfamiliar economy car parked precariously on the edge of the dirt road, near the wooden bridge where he and the double J's had cooled off in earlier years.

Could someone be having car trouble?

He parked the old truck behind the car, and then got out and carefully slid down the bank to the overgrown path along the creek. Man, what a beautiful day for fishing, or just cooling off in the creek. Too hot for anything else. The sun was merciless; the water clear and cool, trickling over rocks. He meandered along the bank toward the deeper pool where frayed ropes still hung limply in the smothering heat. When he saw the old ropes, he realized it had been a long time since they'd had time for such an innocent pastime. He resolved to remove the dangerously worn ropes at his first opportunity.

He turned to continue along the path but stopped short. He saw an empty chair. Slung carelessly over the back of the chair was a blouse and pair of shorts. Shoes lay in the grass under the chair. Uh oh. A woman's clothes and shoes. No woman in them. It was so quiet, he was alarmed and started looking around for the owner of the clothing.

The water parted and a girl rose from the stream with her back to him. His first thought was that he'd dreamed her. Her long, wet hair looked like a waterfall as it clung smoothly to her back. She looked like a nymph or sprite from a fairytale.

Then his vision cleared and she was human. She wiped

water from her eyes with the heels of her hands as she turned and started toward the bank where the chair stood. She wore only a wisp of a lace bra and tiny matching panties. It couldn't have been more revealing had she been naked.

Remy gulped and was unable to look away. He was so taken aback that he couldn't react for a moment. Flustered, he didn't know what to do. But he caught himself and half-turned to go back and pretend not to see her. Then he realized she was bound to notice his cowardly retreat. Better to face it head-on. He stomped heavily down the path like a bull in a China shop so she would have time to react. He cleared his throat, coughed, and came around the bend.

Her deep green eyes mirrored the pool at her back. She looked like the fairytale creature he had first thought her to be. Their eyes met and neither spoke for a moment.

"Well, I guess that answers my question," Remy said.

"What question?" she asked, with a lift of her chin.

Ah, great. She's pissed off, he thought.

"Saw the car back by the road, didn't recognize it, thought someone might be in trouble out here," he said.

"No... Anyway, I don't think so. I just stopped to cool off on my way home," she said evenly.

"I see that. Are you going to be able to get your car back on the road when you're ready to go? It looked like the wheel on the passenger side was over the edge of the shoulder."

"Oh, do you think so?" Her brow furrowed. "I thought I heard a small scrape but couldn't see anything."

"I'll be glad to go back with you and take a look at it," he offered.

"Do I know you?" she stopped. "Aren't you Remington Boudreaux?"

He didn't recognize her. The girl was gorgeous, no way he'd forget that.

"You don't remember me." It was a statement.

"Ma'am, I'm afraid you have me at a loss," he said.

"Sophie Tucker. I was a couple years behind you in high school." Her smile was shy and hesitant.

"No. You can't be Sophie Tucker. You don't look anything like her."

Her green eyes lit with genuine amusement. Her laughter touched him in all the right places. Dammit. He'd been hooked when he'd seen her rising from the water, but her sense of humor was intriguing as well.

"Well, I know I had 'coke bottle glasses' back then and a reputation as one of the smart kids. But, yes, I really am Sophie."

Remy quickly searched his memory. How had he ever not seen this girl? She was a knockout!

He shook his head. "I can only plead the feeble-mindedness of a teenager with way too much to do." He let it go at that.

But she chuckled again. "You're right, you did seem to be in all directions back then. You were dating Maria Lang. How is she doing?"

"Maria?"

"Yes." She nodded.

"No idea." How in the world did she remember Maria, and why did she care?

"Well, don't y'all have kids now?" She seemed surprised.

He hesitated, trying to think of anything his mother might have told him about Maria.

"Maria went off to UT and married a guy there. I think he was fifteenth draft pick by the Titans last year. I don't know about kids, though. That's the word we got from her family."

"Good grief, for some reason I thought you guys were a life-time match. Didn't think you'd break up." Sophie frowned.

"Wasn't a breakup," he admitted. "I couldn't leave the farm long enough to go to UT, so it just worked out that way. Didn't expect her to wait on me; that wouldn't have been fair. Maria always was practical. That's the truth of it."

Remy hadn't thought of the former cheerleader and home-coming queen in years. When he'd had to take over the farm, they'd grown apart. They'd dated for all the important events of high school like homecoming and prom, but he knew he didn't regret Maria's leaving. His life had been so full of work on the farm that he hadn't had time to miss her. Then one day he'd realized he wasn't grief-stricken. He didn't mind being alone. But now he realized he was lonely. Alone and lonely were two different things.

They stared at each other for several silent moments.

She finally spoke. "Oh. Wow." She cleared her throat. "I had no idea. I'm sorry for the assumption. You know the saying, I'm sure."

Remy grinned. "It's okay, I know we were pretty inseparable back then. It was a reasonable question. But after she went on her separate path, I was glad to know she was happy."

Sophie looked at him. "So. How much did you see?"

"Huh?" he sputtered. He had not expected that.

The corner of her mouth quirked. "As in, where was I in the dressing process when you got here? I know your timing couldn't have been *that* good. You looked too innocent."

"Uh, yeah." His whole face flamed. Damn, she'd looked good. But he hadn't wanted to admit he'd seen her.

"That much, huh?" She grinned. "Well, if it's any comfort, I once wore much less for a photo shoot."

Now Remy couldn't have gone to fix a tractor had his life depended on it. Tractor? What tractor? "Photo shoot?" he blurted.

"For a centerfold for a men's magazine."

He stared at her, attempting to get his imagination under control. "What was the magazine?" She named it, and he gaped. "You were in that magazine?"

"Yep," she admitted. "I was 'October Candy' a few years ago."

Remy gulped. He thought his tongue must look like a

necktie and could not seem to close his mouth. Words, drool, none of it. Come on man, zip it!

Sophie let him off the hook. "Actually I'm kidding. I was relying on no one seeing me here at the creek. I was on my way home after years away at school, and simply wanted to cool off and then get back in the car and go home. My AC doesn't work in that old car. I just finished my last year of law school. I worked hard when I wasn't studying, so I've not had a minute to myself in a long time. I rushed right from school to the bar exam and law clerking, but always wanted to come home. Sleep wasn't easy to come by. But I wanted a quick dip before I go home."

"I sure get that," Remy nodded, remembering his own struggle to get an education and run the farm.

"Well, anyway, that cantankerous little car choked all the way here. I had to leave the windows down just to breathe even though dust clouds came in. This red dirt here is either like glue when it's wet or choking you when it's dry. Seems like there's no middle ground. No pun intended. That's why I stopped here. I wanted to cool off for a minute before I went home." She shrugged as she continued. "I applied to Mason and Lee, here in town. When I heard from them after only a couple of weeks, I was stunned. But they called me for a telephone interview. I'm here now for the in-person interview this week. It's a formality, I think. My family goes way back with the Masons. The younger Mr. Mason is now with his father's firm. I think I remember him from school as a spoiled brat. Maybe. I wasn't one of the popular kids, so he won't remember me. But he did sound very nice on the phone. Guess everyone grows up eventually."

Remy thought for a minute and studied her. "You're right. Ron Mason has turned around and become a model citizen. I met him after Dad died and we settled his estate. Ron was very compassionate and helped us make the best of a bad situation.

I'm glad you're home, because now we have another home lawyer who knows the place and folks," Remy adamantly declared. "You're a local. Everyone will be glad to see you. I don't think you have a thing to worry about. You'll be a welcome addition."

"Oh, I hope you're right. I'm heading home to stay with my folks until I have a chance to find my own place. Then I'll prepare for the interview." She sighed. "Now if only that car will get me home."

"I can help make that happen," he offered. "How about we go check out the car? And I can carry your chair?"

She pondered a moment, then smiled. "Well, since you were a decent guy in high school, I'll take you up on the car check. It's been nice catching up with you again. Like all the girls in high school, I had a secret crush on you. I must admit that I'm selfishly glad Maria is happily married."

Remy's face burned. He didn't want her to think he was taking advantage of the situation. He wanted to further the acquaintance. He thought she needed time to realize he was genuinely interested in her. "Well, I'm glad I happened to come by. Maybe after you get settled at work we can go for coffee or lunch?"

Sophie laughed. "Okay, deal. Coffee or lunch it is. I'm eager to catch up on the years I've missed."

Remy gave her a sidelong smile. "I'll be happy to tell you all the news that is news. Lord knows, there's not much in this town."

She giggled. "You might be surprised how much I've missed out on. I may keep you talking a while. I don't know how many of my friends are still here or if I'd recognize them."

His heart leapt. "That's okay with me. My best friends just left for military training, and I'll be glad to chat. We can catch up on who's gone where and done what."

When they reached the car, Sophie started it up and tried to pull away from the shoulder, but one wheel spun in the air while the other flung back dirt and gravel.

"The bottom of the car is resting on the dirt with the other wheel suspended," Remy explained. "But I can fix that. It's not damaged."

Remy pulled his truck in front, hooked a tow chain to the car, and eased her back onto the road.

"That's a relief!" Sophie thanked him. She looked like she wanted to keep him talking like she'd hinted at earlier but didn't. "After all this time, I still can't believe you're the first classmate I've run into."

"Why don't I follow you home just to make sure you get there okay? I won't pull into the driveway but keep going so you can have time with your family while I get the parts to fix my tractor." He didn't tell her that he also wanted to continue talking. He was afraid he'd seem over-eager.

Sophie's eyes were grateful. "That would be a load off my mind."

"Is it okay if I call you in a day or two to check up, and maybe arrange that lunch or coffee?" Remy asked as casually as he could manage. He tried to make himself leave her side window and get into his truck. His feet felt glued to the spot.

She wondered if he could be as interested in her as she was in him. She looked in his eyes and saw the spark she felt reflected there. Her heart sped up. Their eyes held for several moments as they were unable to look away from each other. Sophie blushed and looked down.

"Yes, absolutely," Sophie said fervently. She wrote her phone number on a scrap of paper and gave it to him. They both jolted as their fingers brushed.

With a long last look, Remy smiled gently as he forced himself to leave the side of her car and get into his truck.

Sophie mastered her nerves and drove carefully onto the old road, and headed home, as Remy followed. She kept looking in the rearview mirror to reassure herself he was there and that this was really happening.

She was unaware that Remy's eyes were riveted on hers as if he could see them in the mirror.

They made it to Sophie's family home with no further incident.

Sophie was a little sorry there was nothing to demand his further attention. But she watched as he drove out of sight and waved. She was startled to realize she was sitting dreamily in her car with her hand still frozen in the air long after he'd disappeared.

"Good grief, girl! You're not a teenybopper. Good thing he can't see you," she told herself. "Get out of the car and go in!"

Remy waved as he kept on going to the farm store, with his eyes locked on the sideview mirror. When he got to the store, he sat in his truck for a few seconds. He thought of Sophie's cool green eyes and didn't realize he was sitting in an oven. He glanced up and met his own gaze in the mirror. He had a goofy smile he didn't remember wearing since he'd been a high school freshman. But he wasn't sorry. At length, he got out of the truck and went into the store to get his tractor parts. He didn't know he was whistling.

Later, he repaired the tractor while wearing the same goofy grin. It didn't matter that he'd done no more work that day. Who knew that a day that started out so plain awful could take such a brilliant turn? He couldn't wait to call Sophie in the morning to have coffee. He intended to make it a habit.

The End

ABOUT CS

CS Ward recently retired from the Army as a soldier and as a civilian. Now she enjoys writing fictional tales featuring handsome men, spitfire women, as well as aliens and ghosts rather than wasting time on morons at the office. Instead she immortalizes those morons in her fiction, where she either kills them off in creative ways or makes them slimy cowards stuck forever in that condition. She lives with a menagerie of pets who keep her entertained on a farm in southcentral Tennessee.

REVIEWING THE SITUATION

MARILYN BAXTER

"Ladies and gentlemen, we have a mystery hotel reviewer in the house," the general manager of The Beachview announced at his daily staff briefing.

A collective gasp hissed through the conference room in St. Magnus Island's premiere resort. A mystery reviewer visited a resort, posed as a regular guest, and provided a critique of their visit. A positive review marked a red-letter day for the renowned Georgia establishment.

Kara Benson sipped her fourth cup of coffee for the morning and waited for details. As head of guest services, her job was to make each guest feel as if they were her top priority, which was difficult enough, but nearly impossible when a reviewer was thrown into the mix.

"He checked in for a six-day stay and is in…" Garrett's voice faded as he double-checked his notes. "Suite 38."

Ocean view king. Decorated in blue and sage. Whirlpool tub, sitting area plus balcony, wet bar stocked with…

A thump on the conference table and the sound of her name interrupted Kara's mental inventory.

She made eye contact with her boss. "Sorry, I was thinking ahead."

"Good girl, Kara. That's what I like to see. Initiative. Drive. Team spirit."

"Brown-nosing," someone mumbled.

Kara was used to such comments given the boss was her father. Was it really brown-nosing under those circumstances? The hospitality business was all she'd ever known. Her parents met while working at the Fontainebleau Miami, and she'd been born when they were employed at the brand-new Excalibur in Las Vegas. By her third birthday they'd relocated to Orlando. Kara had grown up in the land of a talking mouse, with summer jobs at the resorts where her parents worked and an expectation to follow in their footsteps.

"...he has the Sunrise Sunset package, so you'll need to schedule his activities and notify all vendors about him. Kara, I want you personally responsible for this man's stay. The name is Thomas or Thompson or something."

The resort was already full because of the upcoming Fourth of July holiday week, and Kara was stressed to the point of living on coffee and antacids. Now she'd have to handle the demands of an overly demanding guest bent on pushing the staff to the limit.

"I have the group from London arriving any moment, and the Truman Bekker family is due around three," Kara explained. Bekker's face had graced the cover of every major news magazine after his company developed a promising new treatment for dementia. "Let Lorenzo take the reviewer," she said, gesturing toward her assistant. "He's more than capable, and since it's an unaccompanied male, Lorenzo would be a better match."

Garrett's glare indicated his displeasure at having his authority questioned. When the muscle in his jaw twitched Kara knew she had pushed too far.

"Lorenzo can manage the London group and the Bekker family. I want you to handle the reviewer. Am I clear?"

Kara snapped a brief salute in her father's direction. Experience had taught her when to back down. As the meeting adjourned, she passed her notes to Lorenzo, then made her way to Suite 38. As she rapped on the heavy oak door, she mentally practiced her introduction, and when the door swung open, she began. "Welcome to The Beachview, Mr....Ben?"

His name wasn't Thomas or Thompson. It was Thompkins. And he was as tall, dark, and handsome as she remembered.

He smiled, then shook his head. "Kara. It's been...a while."

Ten years.

Ten years since he'd graduated and moved across the country. Ten years since the two thousand miles between them ended their relationship.

She bit her bottom lip, nodded, and stared at the floor until she regained her composure. "Welcome to The Beachview," she said haltingly. "I see you have the Sunrise Sunset package. I'll get your excursions arranged ASAP. Any preference on day or time?" She lifted an eyebrow to punctuate the question.

"No. Yes." Ben blew out a long breath. "Let me look at a list of what's available and see if I really want to do any of them. Is that okay?"

Awkward silence stretched between them for what seemed an eternity before Kara nodded in the affirmative. Ben glanced at the t-shirts in his left hand. "Thanks. I think I'll just finish unpacking."

"Of course." Kara turned to leave, understanding Ben had dismissed her like an insignificant servant. "Oh, I forgot," she said, spinning back to face him. "Our Friday cocktail party is at six in the Maritime Lounge. I hope you'll attend."

Ben leaned against the door frame and looked at the t-shirts again. "I didn't bring cocktail attire."

"Not a problem. Island life is casual, so you don't have to wear anything."

Ben chuckled and pinned her with an amused gaze.

"Special. You don't have to wear anything special," she stammered. "Hope to see you there. In your casual attire." Heat crept up her neck as she beat a fast path from the suite.

Dumb. Why not invite him to get naked in the hot tub?

And that thought evoked memories of a weekend in Vail and frayed her nerves even more. But before she could delve further into that memory, her cell vibrated in her jacket pocket. Caller ID indicated her father, a caller she couldn't ignore.

"Have you arranged everything for our reviewer?" he asked without so much as a hello.

"Not yet—"

"Kara, we must impress this man beyond his wildest expectations. We have a reputation to maintain and that won't happen by slacking off. Get right up to his room and make sure his every wish is your command."

"I did," Kara explained with a sigh. "I've introduced myself, told him I'm his beck-and-call girl for the week—"

"You didn't use those words, did you? This man could make or break us, and you're making lewd comments—"

"Dad! Calm down. He wants to settle in before he decides on his activities. And I didn't say anything lewd."

Not too much, anyway.

"Good enough. But don't drop the ball on this. There's too much at stake."

Gathering all her courage, Kara tried once more to extricate herself from the assignment. "I still think it would be better if Lorenzo took over."

"I'm not asking you to sleep with the man, Kara."

Too late. I did that ten years ago.

"I'm simply asking you to do your job."

The irritation in her father's voice was clear.

MARILYN BAXTER

"Send him fishing with the best captain. Line him up with Ross for a massage. Make sure he has the best table at dinner. That sort of thing. Discussion over. And accompany him when you can so he knows he has our undivided attention."

Kara drew in a deep breath trying to control her frustration. "Will do," she said. "And yes, I invited our VIP to the cocktail reception."

"Good girl," Garrett said and then ended the connection.

Kara spotted Ben the moment he entered the lounge. She made eye contact and weaved her way through the room to greet him.

"I see you found the party."

"Mmm-hmm." He nodded toward the man with whom Kara had been conversing. "Since the last name is the same, are you two related?"

"My father. Can I get you something to drink?" Kara asked, quickly changing the subject. Ben hadn't known her father ten years ago and she saw no reason to introduce him now.

Kara led him to the bar where he ordered Scotch and soda. "Easy on the Scotch," he told the bartender. "I've been traveling for two days, and I'm exhausted."

"Two days? You're not in southern California any longer?"

"I am, but I took a red-eye to Atlanta yesterday and then drove the rest of the way today."

"I love the drive once you're off the interstate. I've been here five years, and the scenery still takes my breath away."

"Where were you before?" Ben snagged a canapé from a passing waiter's tray and popped it into his mouth. "Mmm. My compliments to the chef."

"Chicago. It was my first job after graduation."

"There's a big difference between St. Magnus Island, Geor-

162

gia, and Chicago," Ben noted. "I'm too used to moderate climates to go that far north. But the humidity here is a killer."

"I'll share my secret." Kara beckoned with her index finger, and he leaned closer. "Linen," she said in a stage whisper. "Wrinkles like crazy but you'll stay cool."

Ben stepped back and scanned her from head to toe. "If that's linen, you wear wrinkles well."

"This old thing?" Kara laughed, fingering the hem of her bright pink tunic. "Be sure to wear sunscreen outdoors, and you should be fine. And speaking of outdoors, we need to schedule the activities in your package. Would you like to try a fishing trip at dawn tomorrow?"

Ben yawned. "Fishing sounds like fun, but not tomorrow. I'm still trying to adjust to crossing four time zones. And please don't think I'm rude, but I'm going to beg off now, order room service, and go to bed early. Can we discuss it tomorrow?"

"Sure. As a matter of fact, I'm thinking of joining you in bed."

Kara flushed bright crimson, and Ben shook with laughter.

"I mean, I'm going to my own bed. In my room. Alone. By myself," she stammered. "Please let a hole open in the floor so I can crawl in."

"I know what you mean, Kara. And forgive me if I enjoy your awkward moment. I'm usually the king of faux pas, so it's a bit reassuring to see I'm not the only one with foot-in-mouth disease. And with that I'll say goodnight."

***

Kara found a pink message slip on her desk the following morning.

Sign me up for everything. Ben.

Three hours later they headed off on horseback to explore an undeveloped section of beach along with a group from Japan.

"What's next?" Ben asked eagerly as they headed back to the resort.

"You have a massage this afternoon. I figured you might need it after a morning on a horse. Then tomorrow at sunrise I'll drop you at the marina for fishing with the best fishing captain on the Georgia coast."

Ben turned sideways in the passenger seat. "Don't take this the wrong way, but don't you have any other work to do besides hanging with me?"

"Not a thing." Garrett had made it quite clear the reviewer was a priority. "For the duration of your stay, I'm your beck—I mean, I'm at your beck and call."

"Interesting," he said, shaking his head slightly. "And after the fishing trip? Or will I need another massage after that, too? I've been a desk jockey for too long."

"For a desk jockey who seemed reluctant yesterday to do anything, you sure are excited about things now." Of course, that was part of his job as a reviewer. Push the limits, try the patience of the staff, see how good they really were.

Ben shrugged. "It's growing on me. All this fresh salt air, I suppose. My family gave me this trip for Christmas last year, and I kept putting it off. I'm changing jobs, and this seemed a good time for a vacation. If nothing else, my mother will stop nagging. My father died at his desk and..." Ben's voice trailed away, and he turned back toward the car window, staring at the marshland as it whizzed by.

Kara figured the story was a lie, but a reasonable one. She would play along for the sake of the resort and the good review her father expected her to land. They rode the rest of the way in silence, and when she dropped him off under The Beachview's ornate porte cochère, he exited the vehicle without a word.

Kara stood in the lobby at five-thirty sipping hot coffee and waiting for Ben.

"How's our reviewer?"

Kara turned at the sound of her father's voice. "Okay, I suppose. He's not very demanding and hasn't voiced a single complaint yet other than the ungodly hour Arlo starts his fishing trips."

Garrett chuckled. "Early bird gets the worm. Or in this case, the fish. Do you have his week scheduled?"

Kara nodded. "Fishing this morning. Island carriage tour this evening. Paddleboarding tomorrow morning and kayaking the marsh at sunset. And at some point, I'll get him into the spa again."

"Kara, I want him scheduled tightly. I want this man to see everything the resort has to offer. Try hard."

Kara resisted the urge to sigh aloud. Her father believed guests should have activities scheduled every waking minute instead of relaxing on vacation.

"We'll discuss the rest of his stay during lunch." She hesitated a moment, one concern gnawing at her but unsure how her father would receive it. "Are you absolutely positive he's a reviewer? I mean, he doesn't behave like a spoiled child and make unreasonable demands to test us like other reviewers have done." And there was the whole business of their past. Her father hadn't known about their relationship, and Kara saw no reason for him to know she'd slept with the man ten years earlier.

"Without a note from his employer or a t-shirt proclaiming, 'Mystery Reviewer,' there's no way to know for sure. But he fits the profile, and my gut says he is."

Kara's gut screamed the opposite, their college affair notwithstanding. But before she could continue, the elevator dinged, and Ben stepped into the lobby wearing board shorts and a fitted tee. Her hormones screamed even louder. She had found plenty of the resort's male guests attractive; this was completely different. Asking again to have Lorenzo take over was unwise on two fronts: she would be questioning her father's authority again, and she might alert him to her attraction to a guest, which was categorically forbidden.

"Mr. Thompkins! Good morning. I trust your stay is to your satisfaction." Garrett Benson never asked if you were pleased; he told you. "Kara's car is outside, and she'll drop you off at the marina."

"You're not going with me?" Ben asked.

"Not today. This is a private excursion."

Ben shrugged, and Kara could have sworn he was disappointed.

"Actually, I rather enjoy watching newbies disembark and stumble around getting their land legs back," she quipped. "It's better entertainment than television."

Garrett's nostrils flared and his caustic stare could have scorched metal.

"She's good," Ben said with a laugh. "A real smart aleck, but I appreciate that. Keeps me humble."

Kara sent up a silent thank-you. Ben brought out her playful side, but she needed to use caution.

"Shall we go?" She gestured toward the exit. Fifteen minutes later, she delivered Ben into the very capable hands of Arlo Reeves, who had a reputation for patience with even the most inexperienced angler.

Six hours later, a bedraggled Ben posed beside the four-foot-long King Mackerel he'd hooked. "Fishing is hard work," he called out, tugging at his cap and sunglasses, and sending a longing stare at the iced beverage in Kara's hand.

I wish he'd look at me like that.

Kara gave herself a mental kick. As enticing as Ben Thompkins might be, she couldn't afford to lose her job over him. And besides, it hadn't worked out between them a decade before, so why would it work now?

"Arlo told me about his ten-year-old grandson who's already winning tournaments. I think I'm scarred emotionally now."

"People underestimate the strength and skill required for ocean fishing." Kara paused for a breath. "Arlo might make it look like child's play, but there's a lot of work involved to make it look easy, even for a ten-year-old."

"My aching body agrees with you wholeheartedly." Ben stretched and groaned. "Let me sign the papers to donate my catch to the soup kitchen, and we can head back to the resort. And I'll be indebted to you forever if you tell me where I can get some of that." He pointed toward the can Kara held.

"Right here." She shoved it in his direction, and when their hands touched briefly, a sizzle traveled up her arm. She stepped back to distance herself and steer clear of his power source. Avoiding emotional electrocution at any cost was absolutely necessary.

"Don't let me take yours. I can manage to hobble somewhere and get my own."

"While I'm touched by your pathetic whining," she said, "this is yours. I brought it from the resort for you."

Ben's throat worked as he practically inhaled the contents. "You remembered my favorite drink," he said, setting down the can.

I should, since I slept with you for a year.

Kara smiled sheepishly and shrugged. "I remember a lot of things."

"Then you most likely know I'd like to crawl in a Jacuzzi about now and soak my poor body."

"Play your cards right, mister, and I might be able to get you in for another massage."

Ben grasped her hand. "If you do that, I'll love you forever."

"Why, Mr. Thompkins, that sounds like a proposal." Kara

167

batted her lashes and flirted openly. Every gray cell screamed to stop because she was headed for dangerous territory.

Ben cleared his throat, and the moment became more solemn. "I do have a proposal of sorts for you. Will you join me for dinner tonight?"

Yes!

"I can't. It's against policy to date a guest."

"So, who says it's a date?

Anyone watching us, that's who.

As much as she wanted to share the evening with him, Kara knew better.

"You're my personal concierge, aren't you?" he asked holding up one finger.

Kara nodded.

"And you're at my beck and call?" he added, holding up a second finger.

She nodded again.

"Well, I'm beck-and-calling you to have dinner with me to discuss my upcoming activities and how to maximize my time on the island."

In a quasi-logical sort of way Kara agreed that it made sense.

"Then it's settled. I've already made a reservation for seven in the Sandpiper Room. And you don't need to dress up. Remember? Resort attire is casual, and you don't need to wear anything," he added with a wink.

"You're not going to let me live that down, are you?" Ben Thompkins was doing a little flirting of his own. And it was working. Damn it.

They talked and laughed over a meal featuring Atlantic grouper, and the discussion segued from embarrassing moments to favorite movies, and eventually to the sunset carriage ride they

were about to take. The chef had packed a basket with two serv-
ings of his famous peach cobbler and a bottle of Riesling. When
they reached the northernmost end of the island, the carriage
driver pulled into a small park. He hitched the horse and left
them alone to enjoy their dessert under a centuries-old oak
dripping with Spanish moss.

"I saw you at the pool this afternoon," Kara said after several
bites. "And for a desk jockey, you sure moved through the water
well. Your flip turns were pretty smooth."

"Once you learn it, you don't really forget. We used to swim
a lot." Ben took a long sip from his glass of wine.

"We?" Kara asked, not sure she really wanted to know. Had
she been flirting with a married man?

"My wife and son and I," he replied after a long pause, his
eyes growing dark. "We spent a lot of time in the pool or at the
beach. We...." He stared into his wine, then swiped one hand
across his nape.

Kara wanted to know more but wouldn't ask. If Ben wanted
to share, she'd listen but not pry.

"They were headed home from swim class when a drunk
driver hit them head-on. Allison died instantly, but Wes hung
on until the next morning. I buried my family three days later,
and the bastard who killed them didn't have a scratch on him."

Ben dumped the remainder of his wine onto the ground.
Kara reached out and laid her hand atop his.

"I'm sorry." The words felt hollow to her, but they were the
only words she had. Then again, was the story true? Or made up
as part of his cover?

"So you see why I've been married to my job? It's been four
years and all I've done is work six days a week, then go home
and drown my sorrows in reality TV."

"I'm sorry," she repeated, her voice little more than a whisper. "I hope your stay here has helped you relax."

"It has," he said, nodding his head in affirmation. "It's been great, especially seeing you again. You're terrific at your job, and you make those around you feel good. Your family must be proud."

"It's just Dad and me. Mom died right after I finished college." Kara's mother had known about Ben and took the secret to her grave.

"Does it ever get awkward having him for a boss?"

If you only knew.

"Not too often," she lied. "We butt heads on occasion, but he's only doing what he believes is best for the resort."

Ben leaned in and took her hand. "And how about what's best for Kara?"

She wanted to answer that her father often took advantage of her helpful nature and eagerness to please. That she'd let the hotel staff become her family rather than seek a mate and marry. If Ben *was* the mystery reviewer, which she seriously doubted now, he had no need for such personal information.

"As beautiful as this spot is, we really should head back." Kara deftly changed the subject. "We don't want them to send out a search party, do we?"

Ben gathered the picnic basket and helped Kara to her feet. "It's not nearly as beautiful as you." His voice was tender and sincere.

"I bet you say that to all the women," Kara joked.

"You still have no idea how gorgeous you are, do you?"

Kara's breath quickened and her face flushed. She felt wrapped in the invisible warmth of him, and her senses spun out of control. When he stepped closer and pulled her into his arms, her heartbeat stuttered. He framed her face with his palms, leaned in and murmured her name just before his lips captured hers.

The first kiss was surprisingly gentle, and Kara drank greedily, then returned it with a hunger that demanded more. Ben tugged her closer and his hand seared a path down her back.

Their passion grew stronger, then peaked, and the kisses became tender once more. When their lips parted, Ben placed his forehead against hers and whispered her name again. The line between professional and personal had completely disappeared.

Rational thought began to return when she heard the horse whinny. "We should—"

"Yeah, probably, but one more." Ben slanted his mouth across hers and delivered a slow, satisfying kiss.

They rode back to the resort in silence. The horse's hooves and jangling harness beat a syncopated rhythm to the grind of the carriage wheels on the road. When they climbed from the carriage at the resort, Ben reached out, then drew back his hand.

"Can I see you later tonight? Drinks? A walk on the beach? Anything?"

Kara shook her head. "I'll see you in the morning for paddle-boarding."

Ben ushered her up the steps and through the front door, his hand at the small of her back. Kara quickly sidestepped from his touch as her father approached, a broad smile spreading across his face.

"Mr. Thompkins. Good to see you again," he said, shaking Ben's hand vigorously. "I trust my daughter is taking good care of you."

"She's doing an excellent job, Mr. Benson. I can't remember the last time I had such personal attention on a vacation."

"Please, call me Garrett," he insisted, clapping his hand on Ben's shoulder. "The Beachview prides itself on customer service, and I gave Kara orders to take very special care of you and make your stay with us one you'll always remember. Pull out all the stops, I told her. Make him remember the resort and the good times he had here."

Kara watched as Ben's demeanor changed visibly.

"She's certainly gone out of her way to do precisely that." Ben's tone became icy. "You can rest assured, Garrett, that she does a lot more than give mere lip service to your orders."

The veiled reference to their kisses was not lost on Kara, and her stomach knotted when she saw the look of pure disdain in his eyes.

"I'm going to my room now," he said, turning toward the stairway. "Good evening, Garrett. Kara." He dismissed her with a curt nod and bolted up the stairs two at a time.

Kara excused herself as well, but not before hearing one last comment from her father. "He'll give us a stellar review now."

In your dreams, Dad. In your dreams.

When Kara walked into the lobby the following morning, the front desk clerk and two bellmen informed her she was wanted in the main office. Her father's personal assistant wore a scared-rabbit look and told Kara to go right in. No sooner had she closed the door than the bellowing began.

"What did you do, Kara?" he demanded, a scowl souring his face.

"Good morning to you, too," she replied. "And exactly what am I supposed to have done?"

"Ben Thompkins called the front desk this morning and cancelled the remainder of his outings. He asked for all meals to be delivered to his room today."

Kara stood motionless for a few seconds, then swallowed hard. "Perhaps he's tired from the activities so far and wants to rest. I—"

"He specifically asked that we leave him alone." Garrett paced in front of the picture window overlooking the ocean.

"Why do you think I did something? Maybe he simply doesn't want to be smothered by hotel staff every hour of every day. There's nothing wrong with wanting a little solitude."

"He's checking out tomorrow, two days early. What in the hell did you do, Kara?" he repeated.

"I did what you asked. Riding, fishing, island tour, the works."

"That wouldn't make him cut his stay short." Her father crossed the room and gripped her arm. "Something happened."

Kara twisted free from his grasp. "I kissed him, dammit. I kissed him. I might have even let him talk me into more, but you came up after the carriage ride and all but painted me as a call girl sent to make sure he had a good time."

"I was merely letting him know his business was important to us. After all, he's a reviewer—"

"He is not. He's a widower from California," she shouted, making no attempt to keep her voice down. "He's between jobs and his family gave him this trip as a gift. And for your information, we knew each other in college. We were a couple until he graduated and moved across the country. At least he has a life, which is more than I can say for myself."

Garrett stepped back, his brow furrowed. "You have a wonderful life here. Why would you say that?"

"I don't have a life. I have a job. One that makes demands I don't always agree with."

"I only assigned you to take care of Mr. Thompkins to help our rating."

Kara squared her shoulders and stared down her father. "I will not debase myself for this hotel. And don't ever ask me to do it again." She turned and stormed from the office, shaking like a leaf as adrenaline pumped through her veins. And while she still had an ounce of courage in her, she made her way to Suite 38.

"Go away," Ben said after the third time Kara knocked.

"Ben, please. I only need a moment." Just as she was ready to concede defeat, the door swung open. Ben stood in a charcoal, tailored suit with a crisp, white shirt and bold paisley tie. He motioned her in, then shut the door.

"I won't insult you with an apology, but I do want you to know I'm sorry for this misunderstanding. My father was convinced you were a hotel reviewer sent here to rate the resort. I tried to convince him otherwise but..." She shook her head as her voice cracked. "I was just doing my job at first. A job my father ordered me to do. But at some point, it stopped being a job and became.... Seeing you again after so many years was...wonderful."

Ben's posture remained unmoved. Had she really thought she could change his opinion?

"I'm really sorry you were caught in a power struggle," she continued. "I hope you'll reconsider your early departure. Your vacation shouldn't be the victim of the hotel's problems. I've held the suite open should you change your mind. And I'll make arrangements with another staff member to handle any special requests you might have since I'll no longer be employed here."

"Did he fire you?" Ben asked with obvious sincerity.

"No. I've decided to resign."

"Why? You love this job. You told me yourself."

"I thought I did. It's too complicated to explain." Kara moved to the door and grasped the knob. "Anyway, you have a decision to make about staying, and I have a résumé to update and send out."

"No need to do that. Come work with me."

Kara sent him a puzzled look.

"That new job I mentioned? I'm GM at the new lodge on Whelk Island."

Whelk sat across the channel from St. Magnus, visible from the end of the fishing pier. The lodge he referred to was the refurbished Dupree House, a grand hotel built at the turn of the twentieth century. Word had spread through the hospitality industry that it was being brought back to its original glory. Kara's father had even expressed concern it could be real competition for The Beachview.

"I need a head of concierge services, and from what I've seen you'd be perfect for the job. I'm headed there now. Come with me. Look at the property, and we can talk about it over lunch."

"I...I don't know," Kara said warily.

"You just told me you need a job and I'm offering you one. A great one. And besides, this would let me see you every day."

Kara's uncertainty melted. "Well...okay."

As she and Ben made their way through the hotel lobby, Kara noticed her father speaking with a short, balding man who had checked in two days earlier.

"I'm giving this resort an excellent recommendation, Mr. Benson," he explained. "Your staff provided enough attention to make my stay pleasant, but not so much I felt smothered."

"Exactly what I've tried to explain to my father," she said to Ben before dissolving into laughter.

"Looks like your father will get what he wanted after all," Ben said as he reached for Kara's hand and gave it a gentle squeeze.

Kara squeezed back. "It looks like we'll all get our red-letter day."

The End

ABOUT MARILYN

After discovering romance novels quite by accident, Marilyn Baxter revived an interest in writing. Since 2006 she's had over 40 short stories published in the confessions and romance magazines, and in 2013 she sold her first book. She is an active member of her local writing group, Heart of Dixie Fiction Writers.

A native of North Carolina, Marilyn arrived in Huntsville, Alabama, by way of Frankfurt, Germany. She has lived in Alabama longer than anywhere else and calls it home. She raised two great sons and now loves to dote on her three grandchildren.

You can find more from Marilyn at http://www.marilynbaxter.com.

FOUNDERS DAY SURPRISE

JANNETTE SPANN

"Hot guy!"

"Shush, Lexie."

"Hot guy!"

The parrot's wings flapped as she shifted on her roost. "Hot guy!"

Across the street stood an older man, wiping his brow. "Stupid bird. He's only hot because of the weather."

"Hot guy!"

Sally gave the rabbit cage one last swipe with the damp cloth. Cleaning cages was monotonous work, but necessary. It was a far cry from her partnership with her ex-husband in their car dealership in Alabama. Her divorce settlement afforded her the financing to buy Perfect Pets, an established business on downtown Main Street, in Long Branch, Texas. The startup costs weren't bad, but some days, she questioned her decision since it turned out that the street was busy, but not her store.

Animals still had to be fed. She went into the back store-room for a bag of rabbit food and returned to find the puppies barking. "This isn't for you guys."

She dipped a scoop of alfalfa pellets and gazed across Main at the auto parts store. All those men and no prospects in the bunch. Not that she planned to marry again, but if Mr. Right existed, he'd be old and wrinkled before she found him. Her mind was a million miles away when a male voice spoke behind her.

"Jeez!" She jumped, slinging rabbit pellets in the air. With a pounding heart, she turned and collided with the sexiest cowboy she'd ever laid eyes on.

"I'm sorry." The man's apology had a distinct Texas drawl. Laugh lines creased the corners of his blue eyes. "The doorbell chirped twice, you know like a bird, so I thought you knew I was here. Can I help you with this mess?"

"Ah-ah..." Sally stuttered, brain dead. Where was her poise, her quick wit, or even her tongue?

"I was looking for dog food, but... I'll come back later."

He was going through the door when Sally found her voice. "No, come back." But it was too late. He pulled an old Jeep into traffic, as she stomped the floor in frustration.

"Stupid! Stupid! Stupid!" Her one shot at the only hunk in the whole darn town and she'd come across as totally demented. She was too old to swoon, but dang. He didn't have an ounce of flab on that tall, lean body, and those shoulders could block the wind off in a hurricane.

She turned to Lexie. "Idiot bird... what happened to 'Hot guy'!"

The bell chirped when another customer opened the door. Hoping for the tall cowboy, she reminded herself any customer would do. This one wanted mice.

Sally slipped her hand into a heavy rubber glove to pick up the rodents and saw the Jeep pull in again at the curb. White mice were the last thing on her mind when strong masculine legs in tight-fitting jeans emerged from under the steering wheel. Their eyes locked and her heart lunged to the floor, then bounced back into her throat. This stranger was by far the best-looking man she'd seen since crossing the Mississippi. He nodded at her through the plate-glass window, and adjusted the brim of his black Stetson before crossing the street to enter the parts store.

Her imagination ran wild. He was a man of the earth, a rancher...

"I need the mice before Christmas," the woman spoke over her shoulder, interrupting Sally's dream. "If you don't mind?"

"Oh, I'm sorry. I got distracted."

The woman grinned. "Uh-huh. If those jeans look as good coming as they did going, it's worth waiting around to see."

Heat flushed Sally's face as the customer swiped her credit card. "Yes, ma'am."

The lady continued. "How long have you been here?"

Sally smiled. "About three years."

"So, you're an old timer. We've been here three weeks." She held out her hand. "Hi. I'm Heather Smith. My husband is the new high school principal."

"Welcome to Long Branch. I'm Sally Morgan. My sister, Karen, told me they'd hired someone."

Now that her customer had gotten past the initial irritation, Sally liked the woman's friendly attitude.

Heather leaned slightly to the right, a mischievous grin crossing her pretty face. "Here comes your cowboy. Wait. He's talking to an older man. Hurry. Get on this side of the counter."

Sally rounded the corner and recognized Mr. Pearson, the owner of the parts store, as the cowboy removed his Stetson and raked dark brown hair back before replacing the hat. It was him, all right. He stood over six-foot, dwarfing the old guy. Would he come back for the dog food he'd looked at earlier? She could only hope.

"Here." Heather grabbed a pamphlet from the counter and held it up as a buffer so they could watch undetected. "Pretend you're trying to sell this."

Sally's brow scrunched. "You want to buy a manatee?"

"Not in this life."

The cowboy started across the street, pausing long enough for a car to pass. He nodded to the driver, then continued to her side of the road. "Is he coming in here?"

"Well, I hope so. He's got a nice swagger, and you're not wearing a wedding band."

The bell chirped, and Sally's breath came in brief spurts. She froze in her tracks when the cowboy stopped at the dog food section.

Heather shoved her forward. "I'll read this pamphlet while you wait on your other customer."

Although spoken louder than necessary, it spurred Sally to swallow the lump clogged in her throat. *He's just a man—just a man—just a man.* "Can I help you?"

"What do you recommend for a dog that needs a few extra pounds?"

"All Natural is a good brand. Its first three ingredients are beef, chicken, and rice. It also has real dehydrated vegetables."

"Mmm."

His concentration remained focused on the label. She could have been Mr. Pearson and he wouldn't have known the difference. "How old is your dog?"

"I've had him going on six years. His energy level has gone south recently, and I thought maybe changing his feed might help."

"You could try a small bag to see if he'll eat it."

He smiled and returned the larger bag to the shelf. "Good idea. Deputy's appetite has been off lately."

"Deputy? Does that make you the sheriff?"

"Close," he said, following her to the counter with the smaller bag in his hand. "The dog belongs to my nephew. Devin called himself the sheriff, so it was natural he'd need a deputy. When his dad accepted a job in Dallas, they weren't able to take the dog with them."

She rang up his purchase. "I believe they have dogs in Dallas."

"This one isn't friendly with strangers." His laugh was deep and rich. "Deputy is part wolf."

Her eyes widened. "I don't think I've ever seen a wolf dog before."

He handed her a ten and waited for his change. "Why don't I stop by sometime when Deputy's with me?"

"I'd like that."

As the cowboy drove off, Sally realized she didn't catch his name. Would he be back? All Natural was a gourmet dog food, and as far as she knew, no local stores sold the brand, but he could get it online.

Heather spoke from behind her. "How long should that little bag of food last a big dog?"

"Not long, I hope."

She laughed. "He looks even better up close."

"And smells divine, like mahogany, dark teakwood, and something... Did he have a wedding ring on?"

"Not even a trace of an old one. Didn't you notice when he paid for the dog food?"

"Are you kidding? I was so nervous I can't say for sure if I gave him the right change."

"I'd say he's a satisfied customer."

"You think?"

"Well, yeah." Heather picked up her to-go box of mice. "Listen, this has been fun, but it's time for me to start supper. John has a school board meeting tonight, and my boys need their rodents. Good luck with your cowboy."

"Thanks." Sally walked her to the door. "Oh, and Heather. It's good to know I'm not the only one who appreciates a nice pair of jeans."

Her Founders Day plans sucked. Time was running out, and she needed ideas that would bring in customers. She'd met with Karen at her home several times to brainstorm and was interrupted by a different man each time. Coincidence? Doubtful.

After a quick survey of the animals, Sally checked their water supplies and covered the cages. It was near closing when Karen came through the glass door, working the harried and hassled expression well.

"Okay, I'm here," she said. "George is watching our girls, but he isn't happy about my going out tonight."

"It's not like we're doing the town. Besides, this shouldn't take long. Let's go to the back room. I got the portable pens in today." She pulled them from the shipping crate to unfold the prefabricated frames. "Do you think George would mind making reinforcements for the corners? They aren't as sturdy as I'd like."

"Ask him yourself."

"He's your husband."

"So? He's your brother-in-law. Has he ever turned you down when you needed help?"

"No, but I know how hard he works, and I hate to keep bothering him."

Karen's lips pursed. "But it's okay if I bother him on your behalf?"

Sally grinned. "Well, yeah. That's what wives do."

"Then get your own husband again so you can work him to death."

She ignored the comment. If not, they'd be covering the

same old territory they'd harped on for months. Karen meant well, but the dinner dates, or accidental run-ins, and the guys dropping by to see George when a phone call or text would have done, were a bit much. George was a nice guy, but nobody was that popular.

"Justin seemed disappointed you weren't at dinner last night."

"I told you I wasn't coming."

"You're such a pain."

Sally blinked. "Me? I don't want to meet Justin or anybody else you've got in mind. If I'm supposed to find someone, it'll happen."

"But..."

"I'll find my own men, thank-you-very-much!"

Karen followed her to the front and picked up a Husky pup from the pen. "I know."

"Then why don't you butt out?"

"I'm your big sister. If I don't take care of you, who will?"

"What?" Sally's fists propped on her hips. "You're only three years older. Did it ever occur to you I can take care of myself?"

"Sitting at home, night after night?" Karen rubbed the thick fur against her cheek. "This is the most adorable baby. I love her blue eyes."

"So, buy her for your girls."

She lowered the pup back into the pen. "I don't love her that much."

"Why not? You're like a dog with a bone—you just won't let go!"

"That's because I love you. Now, are you coming to dinner Friday night?"

"No. I tried it your way when I first moved here three years ago, remember? You had every Tom, Dick, and Harry that wasn't attached showing up at the feeding trough."

"But…"

"Don't 'but' me. I felt like a prize pig!"

"But a pretty one." Karen's smirk disappeared. "Okay, I'll admit I was a tad overzealous."

"A tad?"

Karen backed off to a safe distance. "I know I've been a little overbearing in the past, but if you'd just meet Justin. Not only is he a wonderful guy, but the kids love him, and he's really smart. He owns a computer consulting firm."

She could just imagine the typical computer nerd her sister wanted to saddle her with. "Ugh. I'm telling you again, give it up!"

"Well!" Karen hurried toward the door. "We'll discuss this when you're more rational."

Sally huffed. As usual, Karen hadn't heard a word she'd said, and still no Founders Day ideas.

Her skirmish with Karen died a natural death, and her dreams of Cowboy, as she thought of him, continued as he visited the parts store across the street. Not once had he darkened her doorway.

The bell chirped as Heather rushed inside. "Man, it's hot out there. Mind if I cool off?"

"Sure."

"What are those guys doing up in the bucket trucks?"

"It's for Founders Day. They're putting special covers on the streetlights to make them look like old-fashioned gaslights."

"Isn't that a lot of work for just one weekend?"

"Long Branch prides itself as a quiet, picturesque town where everyone knows their neighbor. The residential neighborhoods have grown toward Fort Worth, but Main Street is the heart of the historic district. It hasn't changed since they built city hall here in the eighteen-hundreds."

"Historical? I'm surprised there's no hitching posts."

"Those go up tomorrow. The wooden storefronts and sidewalks never change, but inside we're to go all out to set the mood."

"What will you do?"

That was the same question the city council had asked, and like then, she still had no answers. "I've ordered wooden pens to set on the sidewalk and rotate animals in and out during the day."

"Is that all you've got? What about in here?"

Sally's shoulders slumped as she looked around. "I plan to use baby chicks as a drawing card. Did they have pet stores back in the eighteen-hundreds?"

"Who knows?" Heather walked around the store, stopping to measure with her hands. "What customers are you looking for?"

"The kind spending money."

She laughed. "I figured that. Mind if I make a suggestion?"

"Feel free."

She pointed toward the large pictures hanging on the wall. "Where did those posters come from?"

"Me. I'm an amateur photographer."

"Amateur, huh?" Heather pursed her lips and nodded. "You're good. Have you thought about making children's pictures holding an animal?"

Sally shook her head. "They could get scratched or peed on. I'm not sure my liability insurance would cover if I got sued."

"I wasn't thinking lions and tigers, more like kittens and puppies. You'll need a waiver for the parent to sign, but I've got one you can copy. They'll need to give a phone number or email address so you can send the pictures to them. Or the parents can come in to pick up the prints. Might make an extra sale that way."

"That's a neat idea, and I'll hang numbers in the background corner to match the waivers so everyone gets the right picture."

She'd have to check prices with her favorite photo lab about the prints, but the plan was doable. "I'll charge two prices, one for digital and another—plus shipping—if they want prints."

"Anything on sale?"

"Small bags of feed. It's foot traffic only that weekend."

"Speaking of small bags, has your cowboy stopped for more dog food?"

"Nope."

"He will."

Sally refused to talk about a man who wasn't the least bit interested in her. Founders Day was getting closer, and she liked the new game plan. The photos were a good idea, and advertising on the store website and the local paper should give adequate coverage. Then again, she could make flyers for the local bulletin boards and ask Karen to start an online chat with other mothers.

Relaxed against the counter, Heather laughed. "I can see the wheels turning in your brain. Since you have plans to make, I'll go, and let you get busy, but if you need help with promoting, or here in the store that weekend, I'm available."

"You'd do that?"

"Sure. When will you start taking the pictures?"

"As early as possible. Karen has agreed to run the register, and her husband, George, will guard the outside animals. They're all the help I'd planned on, but you're a godsend."

Heather grinned. "Glad to help, and I'll call if I think of something else."

"Thanks, I appreciate it." The extra help should free her to talk to customers and take pictures.

The trick to making Heather's idea work was to keep the expense down, without skimping on quality. She'd save money by designing the flyers and sale posters using her graphic app. Colors had to pop for the flyers to be noticed.

"Not hot!"

Sally jerked her head around to stare at the parrot. In all these years, she'd never heard the bird say anything but hot guy. Outside her window sat the dusty Jeep, minus the driver. She scratched the parrot's purple chest and fed her a seed.

"Hot guy! Hot guy!"

Watching old men did nothing for her. Sometimes being alone sucked, but not enough to consider meeting Karen's computer nerd.

The bell chirped. "Not hot! Not hot!"

Sally's pulse raced when Cowboy opened the door and a massive canine with yellow-gold eyes and lush, brownish-gray fur rushed inside. His owner held tight as the dog strained against the leash, his nose sniffing at the puppies with strings of drool splattering on the floor. She eased around the counter, but a low growl and show of teeth stopped her. "Wow, that dog food must have worked!"

A ferocious bark caused the puppies to tremble and whine.

"Um… Is that his way of saying hello?"

"Sit." The forceful command filled the shop.

Sally thought he was talking to her, until the dog obeyed, adding slack to his heavy leash.

"Shake hands." Her wary expression made the cowboy smile. "You're safe. Deputy isn't used to being inside stores, and most of your animals would be food for him in the wild."

"Oh, okay." She eased closer and let the raised paw fill her hand. "Nice to meet you, Deputy."

The low growling stopped, and his nose flared as he sniffed her. She jumped when his tongue licked forward, just missing her mouth. "What's he doing?"

"Saying hello."

"A paw shake is sufficient for me."

Cowboy chuckled, dimples sinking into his cheeks. "Not to his way of thinking. Wolves run in packs. After they sniff you, they'll bring their jaws close to your mouth and lick your teeth. It's a ritual. If they don't finish, like now, because you moved away, they may try to hold your face with their teeth. After they finish licking your teeth, they expect you to lick theirs."

"That's okay." Sally backed behind the counter. "Just how much wolf is in him?"

He glanced down at the dog. "I'd say low to medium. DNA won't reveal it, but we're estimating his wolf ancestors are five generations back."

"And he still wants to greet like a wolf?"

"It's part of his instincts."

She itched to feel the texture of Deputy's extraordinarily thick coat, but he kept staring at her with those yellow-gold eyes. She wasn't about to move too close in case he tried to finish his greeting. "He's beautiful."

"Thank you. Deputy is affectionate if he knows you, but he doesn't like strangers or kids. That's why I waited to bring him. I figured the store would have emptied for the day. Even though he's well-trained and intelligent, his energy level is returning, and there wasn't time for him to get his exercise this afternoon."

"Wait." She frowned, not sure she understood correctly. "If this breed doesn't like kids, why did your nephew's parents agree to the dog?"

"They thought he was a German Shepherd, which is great with kids. As he grew and started showing wolf tendencies, they became concerned, so I agreed to take him."

"He'll never be mistaken for a lapdog."

"Or a house dog, either. Deputy has an outside enclosure with an exercise area."

"Why does he keep staring at me?"

"Guess he thinks you're pretty. I know I do."

"Are you sure?" A nervous chill ran up her spine. "I mean, I appreciate the compliment, but it's more like he's wondering how many meals I'd make."

He laughed and stepped toward the feed section. "In that case, I'd better get another bag of this and take him home. He eats meat every day, and I'm supplementing with this. I'll feed him before we come next time."

Sally rang up the purchase and glanced toward the wolf dog. His steady gaze had yet to waver. "I'm glad it helped. He's much too pretty to get sick."

"Deputy looks even better in his winter coat."

Sally followed Cowboy and his companion to the door, keeping a safe distance. Dogs were her favorite pets, but this one made her nervous, or was it Cowboy saying she was pretty, and they'd be back? That mellow Texas drawl, along with his sexy grin, brought a smile to her face. She could fall for a guy like him.

Sally geared the campaign toward children, to give them something to remember her store by. In keeping with the town's western heritage, she photoshopped Lexie in a miniature cowboy hat and six-shooter for the handout flyers. A fun poster of the girls sitting in the puppy pen with the kittens, puppies, and rabbits hung outside the store.

"Hot guy!"

"Hush."

"Hot guy!"

"That's enough, Lexie. There's no shortage of old men walking around, and I'm not listening to you all day."

"Hot guy! Hot guy!"

Sally tossed the cloth over the bird cage as Lexie let out another, "Hot...!"

Everyone she'd hoped to see, except her cowboy, had dropped by. He was probably the only man in Long Branch that hadn't visited the parts store all week. She hung the backdrop for the photo shoot out of the way of store traffic, but still conspicuous enough to remind parents to have their children's picture taken. With the disk reflector, speedlight, and tripod in place, she checked her supply of rechargeable batteries and adjusted the shutter speed and lenses on her cameras, along with adding fresh memory cards. The Founders Day Celebration would officially begin on Saturday morning, and she wanted to be ready.

Toe nails clicking on the pine floor got her attention when the bell chirped. Deputy barreled into the shop, pulling his master. "Sit!" The wolf dog was halfway across the store before he stopped. "I'm sorry," Cowboy said, holding the leash with both hands. "I don't know what's gotten into him today."

He pushed the brim of his Stetson back and looked toward Lexie. "Why's the bird covered?"

"Because she can't be quiet."

"Not like other females?" He grinned. "You've rearranged, haven't you?"

"Ha-ha. Not funny, and yes, I made room for a miniature photo shoot. I hope a lot of kids come in."

"That's why I'm here." His right dimple winked. "I saw a flyer and..."

"You want your picture made?"

"Not me. My dog."

The wolf dog cocked his head from side to side, not taking his yellow-gold eyes off her. Although standing perfectly still at the moment, he seemed to have pent-up energy waiting to break loose.

"Sure, if you think he'll stand still long enough." She stepped forward and a low growl made her spine stiffen as she returned the dog's stare. "Now you listen to me, you giant fur ball. This is my store—you're the guest—so act like it!"

To her surprise, the dog stepped aside, allowing her to pass.

A cocky grin split Cowboy's face. "Alpha male just met his match."

"Yes, well," she said, "alpha female is shaking in her boots, so let's get this over with."

He nodded. "Yes, ma'am."

"The name's Sally, not ma'am."

"Gotcha."

Sally moved a second box to make a platform large enough to hold the wolf dog. "Stand up here so I can adjust the setting. He's twice the size of what I was expecting to photograph. Get a tight grip in case the speedlight startles him when I turn it on."

To her surprise, Deputy ignored the bright light and watched the foot traffic passing the door. She got a couple of good shots. On Cowboy's command, he turned to look at the camera. The first pose was innocent, but on the next command, Deputy's head lowered as his muzzle wrinkled and teeth bared, showing two-inch canines that could rip off an arm. Those piercing yellow-gold eyes stared straight into the camera lens, and fear shot through her like a bolt of lightning as her nervous finger took shot after shot of the beast.

"Good boy." Cowboy rubbed his back and the faithful companion licked toward his master. "Do you think we could take the leash off for just one more?"

"Well," she said, glancing at the people passing by outside. "Maybe some other time, but I'd like to get one with his paws on your shoulders. It'll give validity to the wild stories you'll tell about Deputy someday."

He eased the dog from the boxes so Sally could set up for the next shot. Cowboy was well over six feet tall, but Deputy's head was even taller when they faced each other in the first shot.

"Turn this way, both of you." She snapped four shots while Cowboy dodged the friendly tongue. "That's great," she said after getting the pictures she wanted. "I'll see if I can edit out the leash."

The bell chirped and in walked a white poodle, followed by an elderly lady fanning herself with a tissue. "My goodness, this air feels good."

Deputy growled, and Cowboy held the leash with both hands to keep the dog from lunging. "I should get him home before mayhem breaks loose."

The whimpering poodle jumped into the woman's arms.

"I should have these ready by the middle of next week," Sally said, before Cowboy closed the door behind him. "Thank you."

The lady breathed again when they were alone. "Oh, my stars! What was that?"

"A wolf dog."

"Is it legal to have those for pets?"

"Yes, ma'am, but it takes a special person to handle one."

Alone again, Sally thought of Cowboy. She'd given him the perfect opportunity to introduce himself, but it had flown over his head. Or had it? Maybe he wasn't interested, even though today was the third time he'd been alone in the store with her. Then she realized he'd also failed to sign for the photos.

Founders Day arrived sunny and hot. Sally found George leaning against the hitching post, wiping sweat, when she turned the corner. "Morning, George. Where's Karen?"

"Dropping the girls off at the neighbors before getting breakfast."

She inserted the key and flipped the light switch. "I'm starving already."

Heather appeared moments later as George moved the pen

outside. They carried out puppies and rabbits while Sally checked the cameras. The shop had filled with parents and children on Friday afternoon, and she'd called in reinforcements to help. No way could she have handled the crowd on her own.

If Saturday turned out the same, she'd have to order more inventory. Three dogs and five kittens had sold. Replacing them would be expensive, but for the moment, her bank account thrived.

Karen breezed in, carrying a sack of sausage biscuits and four cups of hot coffee. "Breakfast is here."

The first customers arrived a few minutes later, and she slid the unopened biscuit under the counter and began photographing triplets. She'd never dreamed so many parents would pay for amateur pictures. The store cleared at noon when the parade started near what was once the office of Doc Bean, back in the eighteen-hundreds.

Sally wolfed down the cold biscuit, then checked on her less popular animals. "Where's Mandy?"

Heather looked around. "Which one's Mandy?"

"The salamander that was in this bowl."

"He sold."

"You're kidding? I thought I'd have to bury him."

As the parade ended, more customers returned. By midafternoon, her selection of animals was slim. Lexie perched next to the tripod, and whenever an older man came in, the bird's "Hot guy!" put the kids in stitches. To Sally's relief, the crowd cleared earlier than the day before.

George put the remaining animals back into their cages and moved the outside pen to the storeroom. "Anything else I can do?"

Sally slumped. "My feet and shoulders are on fire."

Three sets of tired eyes turned her way... not an ounce of sympathy in the bunch.

"It's been fun," Heather said, "but I'm out of here."

George followed. "I'll get the girls, Karen. Are you buying supper, or should I?"

"You can." Karen leaned on her broom. "I'll help clean up."

"Are you riding that thing home?"

She swatted his bottom. "Get out of here."

"Thanks for the help. I'll pay y'all tomorrow." Sally ran the register tapes, removed the money, and checked the sign-in sheets for the pictures. "I shouldn't have any problem getting the photos to the right parents."

"Good." Karen leaned against the counter, a rolled-up flyer in her hand. "These did the trick."

"Uh-huh."

"I talked with George at lunch."

"And?"

"You've missed your chance with Justin."

"Did I?" She smirked. "Such a shame."

The sarcastic remark got her hand smacked with the flyer. "According to George, Justin has his eye on some woman... seems she's smart, funny, and drop-dead gorgeous."

"Good for him. Maybe I can take you up on a dinner invitation—again—for a little while. Do you remember the kid who bought those chicks at closing time yesterday?"

"Yeah, Lance Matthew's boy. Why?"

"I need to get in touch with him."

A grin crossed Karen's face. "I'll call his dad. It'll give you a chance to meet him."

Sally chunked her pencil in the notebook. "If his dad is single, you can forget it."

Karen huffed. "I promise you, he's not single by choice. His wife died in an accident last year. Since then, it's just the two of them. You could do worse, and you already like his son or you wouldn't be asking about him."

"I plan to give him the remaining chicks if he's got room."

"Consider it done."

Sally shook her head. "I'm serious, Karen. If I want a man, I'll find my own."

"Just make sure he's not another loser."

"My ex didn't exactly have loser tattooed on his forehead."

"I know, Sal. It's just, I want you to be happy."

"Thanks, and no more matchmaking... please!"

Karen jiggled her car keys. "I'll try, but no guarantees."

Alone at last, peacefulness settled in the store as Sally checked to make sure everything was secure. She reached for her purse with the money inside, ready to call it a day, when the bell chirped. Thinking the door was locked, her breath caught, and she eased the purse back under the counter. "Be right with you."

Her stomach somersaulted when twin dimples greeted her from across the room as he walked toward her.

"Hello." Cowboy's deep, mellow voice rocked her nervous system. "Is this a bad time, since you've had such a busy weekend?"

"No, not at all," she said, her heart racing at his nearness. Hopefully, he'd come for something besides dog food, like asking her out.

"My uncle needed extra help in his parts store today, and I saw how crazy it's been here."

"Your uncle owns the parts store?"

"For thirty years."

"That's the busiest store on Main Street."

"He does all right." Cowboy grinned, and she felt herself spiraling toward him. "That's not why I came by."

His calm manner hypnotized. "It's not?"

"No. Your sister, Karen, enjoys playing matchmaker. I've been her prime target for some time now."

"You know my sister?" Sally's hope soared as his grin reached his eyes.

He touched the brim of his Stetson, his dimples winking. "George is a friend of mine, and according to him, Karen's made you gun-shy, so if I'm ever going to meet you, I'll have to introduce myself. I'm Justin Palmer."

The End

ABOUT JANNETTE

A native of northwest Alabama, Jannette was first published in 2012. She's no stranger to heartache, but knows God is in control.

Her Inspirational Romance novels give readers a chance to forget their problems and visit the small southern towns, where her quirky sense of humor comes alive with unforgettable characters.

Visit her Website at

http://www.jannettespann.com/

BEER AND CAVIAR

LINDA HOWARD

The forecast called for snow, and the first lazy flakes began drifting down while Siana Mallory was filling her gas tank. She turned up the collar of her leather jacket against the cold, and began mentally checking her readiness status. Snow wasn't uncommon in western North Carolina and this weather front had been predicted for days—she knew she had plenty of food and cash, etc., but thoroughness was her middle name. This time the forecasters were saying there could be eight to ten inches, which was enough to cause more than a day of inconvenience. As it was Friday afternoon, this was the perfect time for snow, with no school and people off work for the weekend.

The real danger was if the power went out, but she had contingency plans for that, too. Her younger sister Jenni had once told her that she had contingency plans in place if her first three contingency plans failed. Siana had shrugged and said, "Maybe."

Her fourth-in-line contingency plan was to go to her parents' house, but she liked her own space and the peace and quiet of being alone. The only way she'd do that was if her parents needed her, or the whole family converged there, which would turn the atmosphere into a snow-bound party.

"Hey, girl."

She didn't jump at the voice even though she hadn't heard him approach, something unusual in itself because she made a habit of being aware of her surroundings: it was the smart thing to do and she was nothing if not smart. Still, she'd grown up hearing that voice and how it changed over the years, from child to adolescent to man. Months might pass without them seeing each other but that didn't matter. His voice was in her DNA . . . or maybe it was her hormones. What Luke Arledge did to a woman's hormones should be illegal.

"Hey, boy," she returned equably, leaning against her car and crossing her legs at the ankle as she watched the numbers clicking by in the pump screen. She could manage the casual act because she'd had a lifetime to perfect it.

Tall and dark and as graceful as a cat, he leaned against the car beside her. "How's everybody?"

"They're all good—even Wyatt."

Their gazes met and they shared a grin. Police lieutenant Wyatt Bloodsworth was married to Siana's older sister, Blair— and Blair was four months pregnant, meaning she was hormonal (Wyatt's fault), still throwing up day and night (Wyatt's fault), and didn't like the color of her nipples (also Wyatt's fault). Wyatt was handling it all like a pro, depending on the advice of their dad who was just happy to have another man in the family to keep him company.

"How about your bunch?"

"All good. The great bedroom furniture fiasco still surfaces from time to time, which Dad counters with the attack-by-car, then I remind them that no way in hell is Dad moving back in with me to destroy my social life, so if they split up again they'd better damn well get divorced. And you know that isn't going to happen."

Siana laughed. She was relieved that she sounded so natural; Luke was a tomcat, with women sliding in and out of his bed like it was the portal to a dimension made of ice cream. She ached inside thinking of those women, but that ache was another secret and she never let it show. "A man has to protect his social life."

He'd brought up the subject but for some reason her reply made his expression tighten. Most people wouldn't have noticed, but Siana was a lawyer, a damn good one, and reading people was her superpower.

He said, "Blair told me most thinking women would make me microwave my—ah, myself—before letting me touch them. Is that why you've never given me the time of day?" He turned to face her, his dark eyes intense and almost angry.

Almost nothing caught Siana flat-footed, but now she felt like a guppy, her mouth opening and closing without any coherent thought forming in her brain and making its way to her tongue. What finally came out was a million miles from brilliant. "Ahh... *what?*"

"Us. Together. Siana and Luke, sitting in a tree, k-i-s-s-i-n-g. Like the old rhyme, but without the tree crap."

Wildly she looked around, so completely off-balance that she couldn't believe she was standing at a gas station on a miserably gray day, in the cold and blowing snow, while Luke Arledge was saying the most improbable things she'd ever heard in her life. She took a deep breath, and with it came enough composure to actually form a sentence. "You *do* remember the rest of that rhyme, right?"

"*First comes love and then comes marriage, and then comes Siana with a baby in a carriage.* Yeah, I remember every word."

Usually Siana was very composed; this wasn't one of those times. She felt heat rush to her face as fury bloomed in her chest and exploded out her mouth as she rounded on him. "Damn you! I could punch you right in the mouth! How *dare* you throw this at me without even a minute's warning, without working up to it by even asking me out first! You've *never* asked me out! You've been out with every available woman you've ever met except for *me*! What the living hell?"

"I haven't been out with Blair," he countered. "Or Jenni. Have you ever asked yourself why?"

No. No, she hadn't.

"I never wanted to date them. Blair is too much like your mother and I'm afraid of her, and Jenni is too focused on herself. Besides, they're your sisters, and dating them would have forever put you out of my reach."

"You are not afraid of Mom," was the only thought that came to mind.

"Every man who knows her except your dad is afraid of her. He's a warrior. Like Wyatt with Blair, though Blair is so good-natured that isn't a good comparison."

Perceptive. He was frighteningly perceptive. Blair was such a steam-roller almost no one outside her family realized how much fun she had with it.

Carefully, feeling her way, Siana asked, "I'm not sure what's happening here. Are you asking me out?"

The pump had clicked off, and she hadn't noticed. Luke did, though, seizing the handle and pumping those few extra ounces in, then replacing the handle and closing her gas lid. "Would you go?"

"When?"

"Now."

She started to say no, then her heart said yes, then her brain had her looking up at the gray sky, the swirling snow, and saying, "Everything will be closing down, with this snow coming. There's no place to go."

"Go to the lake house with me. Let's get snowed in together, see what happens."

The Arledge family had owned the lake house for as long as

she could remember, and the two families, Arledge and Mallory, had spent many a marvelous summer day there. But it was forty-seven miles away, the last part of the trip was on a narrow, lightly-traveled road that wound up and down some steep grades, and the electricity was almost guaranteed to go off there. "Mom would freak if she couldn't find me—"

"So text her right now and tell her where we're going. I'll do the same with my family."

He was pushing hard, so hard she was kind of at a loss. Luke? Luke Arledge? Yes, he'd been the secret in her heart since they'd been teenagers, over a decade, but she'd never had an inkling that he gave her a moment's thought. There was a lot of details that needed to be unpacked before she could make a rational decision regarding him, but he wasn't giving her the time to unpack even her underwear.

Underwear. *She'd need underwear.*

And with that thought, she knew her decision was already made. Regardless what had suddenly lit a fire under him, she wanted to see where this led. Her ruthlessly practical brain shoved aside the realization that deliberately getting snowbound with him was the most reckless thing she'd ever done, and focused instead on being efficient in her recklessness.

"I'll need to stop by my place to pack."

"So will I."

"Food."

"There are basics at the lake house, but we'll stop at the first grocery store we come to and stock up."

"The power will go out."

"There's a fireplace, plus we put in a generator a few years ago, updated the electrical work and plumbing."

She hadn't known that. She hadn't been to the lake house since she graduated high school. Once she and her sisters had been so close to the Arledge kids that, as her dad had put it, if one of them farted they all smelled it. Growing up had meant they necessarily grew apart, formed separate lives of their own.

"No sex."

His eyes narrowed, telling her he didn't like that at all. They stared at each other for a few minutes, waiting for the other to blink. Siana had built her career on not blinking first. "Okay," he said abruptly. "Not for the first twenty-four hours, at least; if it takes us longer than that to get this thing between us settled, I'll be surprised."

Sure of himself, huh? Yes, he was, always had been; his innate confidence was one of the things that had always attracted her. She shrugged, not leaping at the challenge. "If you're serious about this, we'll take as long as needed."

He whipped out his phone and quickly tapped a few words. "There. My mom knows."

Siana leaned in her open driver's door to filch her cell from the dashboard holder.

Going to lake house with Luke. Will likely be there a few days.

Her phone signaled an incoming text almost simultaneously with his.

Come out a winner.

That was her mom, understanding more than words said, which made Siana wonder how on earth she had given herself away when it came to how she felt about Luke.

"Mom said to be a gentleman," Luke said, frowning at his phone. "When have I not been? I've been so damn gentlemanly it's driven me bat-shit crazy."

"Spoken like a gentleman." She grinned at him, almost giddy because he'd just admitted he'd been pining for her the way she'd pined for him. Mutual pining had to be a good thing.

LINDA HOWARD

She had barely been home for half an hour, just enough time to throw some warm clothes and toiletries into a duffle bag, then change out of her stylish heels and pencil skirt into jeans and boots, exchange her silk blouse for a warm sweater. She watered her house plants, then hurriedly packed a small cooler with snacks and drinks. When her doorbell rang, she was standing ready at the door, duffle bag and cooler at her feet, warm puffer coat thrown over her arm. She jerked the door open before the chime had stopped sounding.

He hadn't changed, but then he'd been wearing jeans and boots anyway. He leaned down to pick up her things, his eyebrows lifting briefly at the sturdy duffle bag. "I figured you for Louis Vuitton, not military surplus."

"We're going to a mountain lake house, not Paris." She set her security system, then stepped out and locked the door.

"True."

"I don't own Vuitton, anyway. I put my money into practical things."

"Like those neck-breaking heels you wear?"

"Those are for intimidating clients and juries." *And jerk bosses,* she thought, but didn't say.

He gave her a curious look as he opened the back door of his huge red dually truck and swung her duffle onto the seat. "Why would you want to intimidate your own client?"

"Too many of them think I can't do an adequate job." She followed him around the truck to the passenger side.

This time his expression was honestly baffled, which made her love him even more. "Why? Because you're a woman, or because of the killer dimples and the boobs?" He made a brief gesture indicating her chest, then opened the door and seized her around the waist, lifting her onto the high seat which she noticed was warm because he'd turned on the seat heater for her.

"Yes." To all of it—and she was tired of fighting that battle.

"Idiots." He closed the door and hoofed it around to the driver's side, swinging up into the seat without any effort. "Not that your dimples *aren't* killer, and for sure God used your breasts as the prototype for what boobs should look like."

"You've never seen my boobs."

He merely lifted his brows as he started the big engine and pulled away from the curb. Siana began wracking her brain, trying to remember a time when he could possibly have seen her naked, or even half-naked. Growing up together meant there was a lot of territory to cover but she came up blank, so she poked him in the ribs. "Give."

"You know most teenage boys are perverts, right?"

"That's a given, so yes."

"We were at the lake house one summer, and you were in Tammy's bedroom changing into your swimsuit. The curtains weren't drawn all the way, there was the dresser mirror, and let's just say I had to go walk in the woods for a while before I was fit for anyone to see me. You were a boy's wet dream come to life."

"My God, how old was I?"

"Fifteen. Sixteen. Something like that."

The timing kind of stunned her, and she sank back against the big leather seat. She'd been fifteen when she'd first developed a crush on him. Being practical despite her age she'd expected the crush to go away. It hadn't. Over the years it had strengthened every time she'd been around him, the roots growing and spreading, digging deep into her heart. She'd dated other boys and men, of course, even actively tried to form romantic attachments to them, but nothing had worked. For her, it was Luke or no one. She'd become resigned to having no one.

He whipped the big pickup into a grocery store parking lot, jumped out and came around to help her out. "Shop like the place is on fire," he said. "I want to be back on the road in fifteen minutes."

The grocery store was, of course, almost a mob scene with everyone doing the same thing, trying to stock up before the snow. Getting out in fifteen minutes meant most of that time would be spent standing in the checkout line, and even the self-checkout lanes were crowded. But Siana liked a challenge, and the fire of battle lit her blue eyes as she grabbed a cart. "Get your own cart," she instructed. "You take aisles one thru seven, I'll take eight through fourteen."

"You've got the booze aisle!" he threw at her as he seized a cart and headed to the produce section.

"I know what you like," she threw back, and charged forward.

It was a competition; she knew it was, because he'd always been the most competitive of his siblings—a product of being the middle child—but she was a middle child too and she went down those aisles like she was in charge of gathering supplies for a war that would start in fifteen minutes. She had some training in this because her work schedule was heavy and she had limited time to spend on the necessities. She grabbed and tossed as she plowed down the aisles; other people pulled their carts to the side, and for those who were oblivious as they parked their carts on one side as they themselves stood on the other side of the aisle studying the various brands of oatmeal, thus blocking the whole aisle, she slowed down long enough to move the carts out of her way.

The milk was already gone, as well as the loaf bread; she'd expected that. Instead she grabbed heavy whipping cream, refrigerated croissant dough, cheese of any kind, sugar, vanilla extract, spices—as well as toilet paper, tissues, and paper towels. Luke would have the canned food aisles and she hoped he thought to pick up some canned meat other than Spam. She zipped down the booze aisle, grabbing beer, pretzels and chips, several dips and salsa, some wine. Eggs! There was a single carton of eggs left, at the back of the top shelf. Without hesitation she climbed up on the edge of the refrigerated section and stretched to snag the carton.

"Damn," said a woman standing on the other side of the aisle. "I wish I'd thought of doing that."

Siana looked around with a smile, saw the two kids climbing on their mother's cart, and immediately handed over the eggs. "You need them more than I do," she said, and took off again. She and Luke would be fine with peanut butter and jelly toast for breakfast.

She skidded into place at the end of the shortest line, and bumped Luke's cart as she did so. "We'll call it a tie," he said, perusing the contents of her cart while she did the same to his. She was glad to see a can of beef stew and, glory hallelujah, a pack of bacon. He checked the time on his phone. "Eight minutes."

"There's no way we'll get out of this line in seven minutes."

"Probably not, but the shopping is the game." He narrowed his eyes at her. "You aren't even breathing hard."

"I do this all the time."

"Of course you do," he said, grinning as he transferred his shopping booty into her cart. "So do I. I always have somewhere else to be and not much time to get there. Usually if I can't get it at a convenience store or a fast food place, I don't eat it."

"I stock up on microwave dinners." Obviously they both had terrible diets—though she did try to have a salad once a day. Prepackaged salads counted, right? And she loved fruit. She hoped Luke had picked up some fruit, but she hadn't spotted any while he was transferring items to her cart.

She watched him as he took his empty cart back to the front of the store, leaving her in place. She wasn't the only woman who watched him, she noticed. Women had always watched him. He was good-looking, but not drop-dead handsome. It was his confident masculinity that drew the eye, the sexy saunter of his gait, the slight swagger that said he could deliver everything he promised—and those dark eyes promised a lot. Her heartbeat changed to a slow, languorous thudding as she thought of perhaps having all those promises for herself.

Perhaps. That was the kicker, that she didn't know for sure if or what he was promising. A fling? No thanks. No matter what pleasure he could promise and deliver, she wasn't settling for anything temporary.

Did he know that? If he didn't know now, she'd make sure he did before things got very far between them. That might make for an uncomfortable atmosphere if they were stranded at the lake house, but they were both adults and could, would, handle it.

The checkout line edged forward. The woman she'd given the eggs to took up position at end of the next line over, and gave Siana a tired smile and a mouthed, "Thank you." Siana smiled back. Feeding kids took priority.

Luke returned, put his hand on the cart handle and subtly edged her to the side. She was glad enough to let him muscle the cart, if he wanted. She stood close enough beside him that her shoulder brushed his arm, the slightest of touches, but it thrilled every cell in her body. How many times as a teenager had she almost made herself sick with longing whenever he touched her while they were swimming in the lake, or playing football, pool, silly card games? The feeling was still the same, the almost giddy pleasure of being close to him.

She loved him. She'd always loved him, and it looked as if she always would.

They were well past his fifteen-minute limit when they finally reached the cashier. She dug out her wallet to pay half, but Luke shot her a semi-thunderous look as he pulled out a credit card. "No," he said when she opened her mouth. "A man takes care of his woman."

The cashier, a young woman with purple streaks in her hair and a tiny gold ring in her nose, blinked and stared at him in astonishment, then quickly looked at Siana, then back at Luke. She never paused in her automatic movements, sliding items in front of the scanner, pushing them toward the array of plastic bags.

"I'm not your woman," Siana calmly pointed out.

"Yet. And you never will be if I don't do things right. I watched your mom operate all my life. You think I didn't pick up pointers?"

She laughed, because her mother was a force of nature, and while it was true her dad all but turned cartwheels to keep her happy Siana knew that her mom returned the favor. Each of them worked to keep the other one happy. It was a good, solid, loving relationship, and while she didn't need one to be identical to theirs she did want the basics, the loving respect and care.

Because the store was so crowded, Siana helped things along by sliding past the cart to begin bagging items herself. "Thanks," the cashier said. She blew her bangs upward in a flutter of purple. "It's been a madhouse in here since the noon forecast. I'm surprised there's anything left to buy."

"No milk or bread left. Or eggs." Siana kept bagging. "There's plenty of produce, though."

"I got us some oranges. And straws." Luke shared a smile with her. Good; he'd gotten fruit, and oranges were her favorite. As kids they'd loved pressing the oranges to release the juice, then jamming a straw into the orange to suck it dry. Siana had the feeling that if her mother was there, she'd be giving Siana a big thumbs-up behind Luke's back, fully approving of his actions so far. He'd been bold, he'd been decisive, he'd been both honest and somewhat sentimental, all of which ticked the right boxes.

She walked beside him as he steered the cart to his truck.

"You do know the moms are already on the phone planning—well, Lord knows what they're planning." She *did* know, but was hesitant to say it out loud. For heavens sake, all they'd done was agree to talk to each other.

"They're planning our wedding and the christening of our first baby," Luke replied. He looked downright happy as he loaded the groceries into the back floorboard of his truck.

Yes, that was exactly what she'd been thinking. Hearing him say it aloud was a bit jarring, though this was the second time in the last hour he'd mentioned weddings and babies.

"Doesn't that scare you? At least make you nervous?"

"Nope. That's kind of the outcome I want."

Jarring escalated straight into *falling off a cliff*, but she kept her voice level. "Kind of?"

"I don't care if there's some variation, as long as I get the main prize." He opened the truck door and lifted her onto the seat. Then he leaned forward and kissed her, for the first time ever.

His kiss was worth the wait, and at the same time made her furious because he could have been kissing her for *years*, and instead for some as-yet-unknown dumb ass reason he was just now getting around to it. She responded by kissing him back with everything she had, tongue and teeth and arms around his neck, leaning into him so her breasts were against him, giving him the fire and need and lonely heartache that had filled her for so many years. She reveled in his taste, his scent, the feel of his arms clamping around her. She rejoiced at the rough sound he made, the way he crowded forward as if he intended to crawl on top of her right there in the grocery store parking lot.

She'd said "no sex," but she wasn't completely certain she'd stop him if he did.

Luckily she didn't have to test her self-control, because he slowly released her, lips and arms, and eased back. "Lord have mercy," he muttered under his breath, resting his forehead against hers. "We'd better go."

Her arms were still around his neck, and she tilted her head to bite his earlobe. "Yes."

"Then stop doing that."

"Okay." She sat back and calmly buckled her seatbelt, though she gave him a sideways glance that had him swearing softly as he closed her door and went around to his own.

He didn't talk as he negotiated traffic, maneuvering the big pickup through the combined late-afternoon and snow-is-coming heavy traffic. The snow was coming down faster, and the ground was beginning to turn white. The streets and roads were still good, retaining just enough of the afternoon heating to keep ice from forming. In an hour, she thought, that situation would likely be different. In an hour, though, they would be at the lake house.

Once they were out of town the road conditions steadily worsened, but the four-wheel-drive handled it without sliding. Siana sat quietly, enveloped in the vehicle's warmth, listening to the swish of the big tires on the pavement. Snow began collecting in the evergreen boughs, heavier and heavier as they left the main road and began climbing into the mountains where the high lake was located. There were no white-knuckle moments, just the sense that she was heading toward the most wonderful adventure of her life.

Darkness, hastened by the cloud cover, fell while they were still in the mountains. The headlight beams picked up the swirling snow, making it look thicker than she knew it was. Snow began accumulating on the windshield and Luke turned on the wipers. His expression, stark in the dashboard light, looked calm and content.

Then they were there. He turned left into the driveway, drove past a curving line of blue spruce, and the house came into view. It was one story, with a porch all the way across the front and wrapping around one side. There wasn't a garage, but it did have an attached carport wide enough to accommodate two vehicles. After parking, Luke lifted her down then went up the three back porch steps to unlock the door into the mudroom. He reached inside and flipped the light switches, illuminating not only the mudroom but the porch and the carport.

The inside of the house was chilly but not freezing. Siana knew her way around as well as she knew her own place and she continued into the kitchen and the cozy great room, turning on lights, going to the thermostat and turning up the heat setting. Within seconds she heard the welcome sound of air moving through the vents. To give the heating system a boost she also turned on the gas fireplace before going back outside to help him bring in the groceries and luggage.

While he was bringing in the last of it she hauled her duffle to Tammy's bedroom, where she and her sisters had always slept, four to the bed, lying across the bed so there was room for all of them. It hadn't changed much. The bedspread and curtains were different but the furniture and its placement was the same. She unpacked, hanging what needed hanging and placing the rest of it in the dresser. Looking up into the same dresser mirror in which Luke had seen her naked breasts while she changed clothes, she smiled. She wasn't as athletic and amusing as Blair, or as pretty as Jenni, but she did have really pretty breasts—to distract men from her shark brain, Blair had once said. She was good with that.

"I don't know about you," Luke called from the kitchen, "but I'm starving. Beef stew all right with you?"

"Sure," she said as she joined him. He had already opened the big can of stew and was dumping it into a pan. While he was doing that Siana unpacked her cooler, storing the drinks in the fridge, snacks in the big snack bowl on the counter, then finished putting away the groceries they'd bought.

She could wait for him to bring up the subject of "us," thereby steering it in the direction he wanted, or she could ask the questions she wanted to ask without waiting for an opening. She hadn't gotten where she was in the law firm by sitting back and waiting, had she?

"So why didn't you ask me out? And when did you decide you wanted to?"

"Second question first: when I saw your breasts in the mirror." He glanced over his shoulder at her as he stirred the stew. "World class."

"Wow. That long ago?" She scowled at him, because at fifteen she'd been dying for him to ask her to his junior/senior prom, either that year or the next—and he hadn't. She couldn't remember the name of the girls he *had* asked, but it certainly hadn't been her.

"I was sixteen. I wasn't given to deep thoughts. I guess I was afraid asking you out would be weird, given that we grew up together and our mothers are best friends. I could just hear the teasing from all sides. And what if we dated for a while and then broke up? What about our families then? Would there be hard feelings, arguments? I didn't want all of us to stop hanging together."

Okay, she could see that. As he'd said, he'd been sixteen. If she'd gotten that far in her own thoughts, she might have had the same reservations.

"And since then?"

"We went in different directions. You went to law school. I got a two-year degree and went into construction."

"You own your construction company," she said pointedly. "I don't own a law firm. I work terrible hours for someone else." And he was young to have his own company, so he wasn't exactly an underachiever.

"Apples and oranges. I work with my hands, you work with your brain. For a long time it was easier to see other women."

"Easier." She almost spat the word. "So what's different now?" She was surprised by the deep core of anger that his actions today had unsealed. Being sixteen was one thing; neither of them was anywhere near sixteen now, and all those years had been wasted. Maybe they wouldn't have worked out, but at least they'd have tried, and known the outcome.

"The other women didn't work. No matter how pretty or how intelligent they were, or how sweet their personalities were, they weren't you. I've known you all your life and no one else is you. I've seen you crying with snot running from your nose because you fell down and skinned your knee—"

"That applies to all of us."

"Yeah." He tilted his head, those dark eyes smiling at her. "It's special. We swam together, we played hide-and-seek together, you hit me in the head with a softball—"

"On purpose, because you pulled Tammy's hair."

"I'll be damned. That was on purpose?"

"If intent matters—and in law it does—I threw it at you because I wanted to hit you. Hitting you in the head was a happy accident."

"I didn't think you were that good."

"Is that why you never chose me for your team?"

"I didn't choose *any* of you girls whenever it was my turn to choose the team. But if I had, it would have been Blair."

"She'd have hit where she was aiming, but it wouldn't have been your head."

He laughed, and despite her lingering anger she had to join him. Shared childhood memories were a permanent link between them, between all the Arledge and Mallory off-spring. There was no getting-to-know-each-other phase because they couldn't remember when they *hadn't* known each other. She knew his temperament—fairly even, but when he got angry, he was *really* angry. She knew his favorite color—red—and his favorite sports teams. She knew some of his favorite foods, though she suspected he might not be as fond of spaghetti now as he had been when he was ten. He likely knew all the same things about her.

"It's always been you." He turned around and leaned against the cabinet, crossing his arms and glaring at her as if all of this was her fault.

She mirrored his position and expression, glaring back. "Nothing has changed."

"Damn it, I know that."

"Except you're about to catch your shirt on fire, if you don't move away from the stove."

He cursed and moved to the left, away from the gas flame. He gave the stew a cursory stir. "Almost ready. It's starting to bubble. Do you want to sit at the table or in front of the fireplace? We can take this up again while we're eating. I'm starving."

"Duh. Fireplace." Their parents had always had the table when both families were there, while the eight kids had sprawled on the floor, over the couch and chairs, anywhere they could find a flat surface to put their plates.

"I'm slightly more civilized than I used to be." Reaching into the top of a cabinet, he took down two trays and set them on the countertop. Siana got napkins, bowls, and spoons.

They settled in front of the fireplace, with their trays on the coffee table. Siana turned on the big-screen TV mounted over the fireplace so they could catch the latest weather forecast. *Winter Storm Warning* scrolled across the bottom of the screen. The TV was satellite; if the snow got heavy they'd lose the picture, but for now everything was still working. They ate in silence, listening to the forecast, looking at the predicted snow accumulation for their area—which was several inches more than predicted the last time she'd checked.

"Good thing it's the weekend," she finally said. "We might get out of here by Sunday afternoon."

"Or not," he said, and sounded as if that would be totally okay with him.

She wasn't surprised. Luke's reputation meant he likely thought he could convince her to abandon her "no sex" stance. Maybe he could, she admitted to herself. But maybe he couldn't, because she wasn't reckless and she hadn't made up her mind to grab at this chance with him. Not that she didn't want to—she did—but a lot of water had passed under their bridges. Luke had been in bed with a lot of women. She didn't know exactly how many "a lot" was and didn't want to know, but she did know she resented each and every time he'd had sex with someone other than her. Being filled with resentment wasn't a good way to start a serious relationship with him.

He still had some reservations, too; that much was obvious. She was glad he at least wanted to move forward despite his reservations. She did, too.

"I don't like my job. I'm thinking of quitting, going out on my own. I haven't told anyone else." She poked her spoon at a piece of carrot in the stew.

He took a bite, nodded. "I can see that."

She was mildly surprised. "Why? It's a sizable firm, pulls in a lot of influential clients."

"The brain I mentioned? That. If your bosses don't appreciate you, why not set up your own firm so you can do what you want, take the cases you want?"

"My income will do a nosedive."

He snorted. "I know you. You've probably been planning this for a couple of years at least, and putting money aside."

That was exactly what she'd been doing. A feeling of warmth spread through her, and it wasn't just the stew hitting the empty spot in her stomach.

They finished eating in silence. Siana's insides were quivering from the sense of being on a precipice, about to step off. Her life was changing, right now. She wanted to slow things down and think about every little detail but suspected this was one time when she needed to put her brain in neutral and go with her emotions. She wanted to hit him. She wanted to jump in his lap and kiss him until they were both crazy.

And . . . right on cue, her brain re-engaged. "I'm not on birth control."

He'd been about to get up, but at her words he sank back on the couch. His dark gaze locked on her face. "Ah . . . good thing you told me. I don't have any condoms with me."

Her mouth fell open as they stared at each other in the flickering firelight. "What? *You* don't have any condoms?" Not that she'd made up her mind to fall in bed with him right now, but she'd thought it best to address birth control before things progressed to that point.

He shrugged. "I haven't needed any in a while."

"How long is 'a while?'" She was a lawyer. She needed details, not generalities.

"Six months or so."

"You haven't had sex for six months, or the women you've been with were on birth control?" She suspected the latter. She *strongly* suspected the latter.

"No sex. I haven't been interested in anyone."

"But you came up here with me intending to have sex if we came to an agreement?"

He looked a little astonished at his own oversight, too. "I guess I was focused on other things, Madam Prosecutor."

"Grocery shopping?"

"I love you. Talking you around was all I had room for in my head."

I love you. He'd said it. And he meant it; she knew every nuance of his expression, the tones of his voice, and he meant it.

Her lips trembled. "I love you too. It was always you."

"Yeah. It was always you, too." He shoved his hand through his dark hair. "Do you think you can be happy with me? I'm on the rough side, I come in dirty from work every day—when there's work, because construction can be an off-and-on thing. I'm in good shape financially for now, but I can't guarantee it."

"I'm going to quit my job," she pointed out. "Ditto."

"I'm beer, and you're caviar."

That was how he saw her. Despite their growing up together, despite him seeing her with her nose running from crying, he saw her as fancy. Siana laughed, though the laugh caught on a tiny sob. "I can't believe you." She stood up and held her hand out to him. "Come on, I want to show you something."

He stood, his big hand wrapping around hers. "If the something you're going to show me involves taking off your clothes, remember the condom situation."

"It doesn't. We can wait." She pulled him toward the kitchen, opened the refrigerator door. "You weren't paying attention when I was unpacking my cooler, but I brought my own drinks in case the grocery store had been wiped clean. What do you see?"

He stared into the cold, brightly lit interior of the refrigerator. "Beer." He shifted the stare to her. "PBR. You drink Pabst?"

"My drink of choice. And I don't care for caviar."

The End

ABOUT LINDA

Linda Howard is an award-winning writer who has appeared on the New York Times Bestseller List, the USA Today Bestseller List, and Publishers Weekly Bestseller list. She sold her first book in 1980, back when the universe was new and dragons flew. She has been married for many years, has grandchildren and great-grandchildren, and lives in Alabama with her husband and a Golden Retriever puppy.

lindahowardbooks.com

AFTERWORD

I hope you've enjoyed our collection of short stories. We certainly had fun writing them!

To find out more about our group and our authors we invite you to check out the Heart of Dixie Fiction Writers webpage, or our Facebook page. We'd love to see you there.

Linda Winstead Jones

https://heartofdixiefictionwriters.com